Collected Short Stories Of Mystery, Romance, And The Occult

by

Amanda Brenner

Table of Contents

Brief descriptions:

<u>Temporarily Away</u>

When a fellow writer's mail is returned marked "Temporarily Away" and she is unable to reach him, Henrietta Harcourt asks the local sheriff to investigate, and the man's mummified remains are discovered in his remote cabin on the edge of a national forest. After his death is dismissed as natural causes, a suspicious Henrietta prods the sheriff to look at someone with motive, means, and opportunity. When he does, "natural causes" begins to look as unlikely as "temporarily away."

<u>Call To Duty</u>

Rick is looking forward to the next phase of his young life and sharing some exciting news with his girlfriend, Cassie. When she calls asking to meet at their favorite hangout near her home, he drives through the dark, rainy streets to the burger joint across town, wondering what could be on her mind. Probably just another of her dramatic fantasies; he's used to them by now. Surely nothing more than that...right?

<u>The Case Of The Pilfered Painting</u>

"Yes, yes," Henrietta said impatiently, fingering the pince-nez that hung from her neck on a black braided cord, "but it's really just too intriguing. It has all the ingredients of a first-rate crime novel, if you ask me. Think of it: a young heiress alone and grief stricken after the mysterious death of her aunt; a painting, a treasured legacy, missing; the police baffled." Then she said solemnly, "You know, Joshua, it just struck me. What if there's a connection between Mrs. Harper's death and the disappearance of that painting? Do you suppose that's possible?" she asked, her eyes wide, her mind focused on the one point of information that would not allow it to rest: Who did it?

<u>A Change Of Plan</u>

Two down-on-their-luck cowboys decide their lives need a change of plan.

Covenant Of Blood

How many were there? Enough. Over the centuries they had evolved to satisfy their needs with a more passive source of the nutrients they required; after all, blood was blood. But not for all. Some could not resist the ancient urge to satisfy their blood lust with the warm, flowing liquid of a living being. In those instances, errant members of the Network were tracked by the death squad known as the Shield, from whom there was no escape. Jordan lived within the guidelines of the Network, as did most of his kind, in present day Baltimore. But his friend, Cam, could not resist the stirrings that drove him to unspeakable acts and attracted the attention of the Shield. When he turned up on Jordan's doorstep asking for help—would he get it? Would Jordan, warned that he himself was under surveillance by the enforcement arm of the Network, dare violate the rules by which his kind had managed to secretly co-exist with the Others? Or would he abandon his friend to his fate? He didn't know, and time was running out.

The Last Cookie

A narrative account of an urban raccoon relocation effort.

Jaded

A struggling private eye finally gets a client, an appraiser for a local art gallery. The woman appraised a valuable vase and the gallery sent it to a collector who agreed on a price based on her appraisal. When the package is received, instead of the valuable Ming rose jade vase it should have contained, there was a plastic replica. Our detective is hired to find out what happened and who engineered the switch.

- Temporarily Away -

Henrietta Harcourt considered the piece of mail in her hand, puzzled by the postal notation that accompanied its return. "Temporarily Away," it said. It was the latest journal of club activity published and distributed to members of her writers' group, The Grey Goose Quill Society. This particular copy had been sent to Matt Mercer in Pleasant Corners, a small and obscure rural community about thirty miles from Henrietta's home in Dobbsville.

Temporarily away? Like where? As secretary for the group, Henrietta was in charge of the membership rolls; in fact, it was her job to keep track of the group's small cadre of writers, some successful but mostly amateurs wishing they were.

She decided she would simply send him a message alerting him to the situation; after all, he was entitled to the Society's quarterly journals as part of his membership fee. And so she promptly sent a message to the web address on her record roll, confident the mystery would be cleared up as soon as he received her explanation. Several minutes after dispatching the missive, it was returned bearing a notation that there was no such address!

Henrietta stared at the rejection a full minute before picking up the telephone and dialing the number Matt had provided on his membership application. Six rings later, the call rolled over to Matt's answering machine. There was nothing unusual or informational in his invitation to leave a message which he promised to return promptly, yet six hours passed with no word.

At this point, Henrietta pondered her options. Since she had no idea of how long Matt had already been gone, she considered simply remailing the journal, but on reflection, considered that if one piece had recently been returned because he was "temporarily away," there was no guarantee that a second attempt would be successful. Consulting her records, Henrietta noted there was no alternative 'snow bird' address for Matt, as was the case with several other members who wintered in sunnier climes. No clue at all. If he had arranged for his mail to be held at the post office during his absence, the journal, being first class mail and bearing a return request in case of address change or inability to deliver, still would have been sent back. Then a thought occurred to her—if the post office knows Matt is "temporarily away," perhaps they also know when he will return.

Dialing the Dobbsville post office, whose jurisdiction included the tiny hamlet of Pleasant Corners, resulted in the call being answered by Billy Bertram, one of three employees in the small branch office of the town of three thousand.

"Billy," she began, "I just received one of the journals from a recent mailing of our writers' group. This one was addressed to Matt Mercer in Pleasant Corners. It had a yellow sticker with the words 'temporarily away' on it. I'm not aware of any other address for Matt, so can only assume he is perhaps away on business or vacation. In any case, can you tell me when he's expected back? I'm sure he would wish to receive his copy, but I'd prefer to know when he is expected back before I send it out again."

She heard Billy mumble something that sounded like, "jus a minute," and a loud clap as he set the receiver down on the counter. She waited. Several minutes went by while voices and music sounded in the background. Then the receiver clanked again as someone picked it up. It was Marge Morgan, the postal supervisor. "May I help you?" she said politely.

"Marge? It's Henrietta Harcourt."

"Oh, yes, Henrietta—what can I do for you?"

Henrietta repeated what she had told Billy. "Have you any idea when Matt is expected home so I can forward his journal?"

"Actually, Henrietta, as far as we can tell, he *is* home. We have no instructions to either hold or forward his mail."

"Well, then," Henrietta said carefully, "why would his journal have been returned with the notice of "temporarily away?"

There was a short silence on the other end of the line before Marge said, "Hold on a minute, Henrietta, the carrier on Mr. Mercer's route just came in from his rounds." Expecting another clang when Marge laid the receiver on the counter, Henrietta instead listened to muffled voices in a back-and-forth conversation. Apparently Marge was holding her hand over the mouthpiece while she questioned the carrier. There was another short silence before Marge resumed their conversation.

"Henrietta?"

"Yes, Marge, I'm here."

"Well, it seems that Matt is simply not collecting his mail. It's been piling up on his front porch for the past week. The carrier assumed he was just away for a few days and continued to add his mail to whatever had been previously delivered. The journal you received was returned because of the instructions that if it cannot be delivered it is to be returned to sender, and the return address on the envelope was yours."

Of course it was mine, Henrietta thought irritably. Do they think the printer's address would have made more sense? But all she said was, "I see. May I ask how long you will continue to let his mail accumulate before notifying someone that something is wrong?"

"We don't know if anything *is* wrong. He could simply be gone and didn't think to make arrangements for his mail. It's really not unusual, Henrietta." Now Marge's voice had a "it's really none of your business, you nosy old bat" tonal quality. Henrietta recalled something about discretion being the better part of valor and said simply, "I understand. Well, thank you, Marge, for looking into it. I'm sorry I bothered you. You're right, of course." Hoping she had sufficiently mollified the supervisor, Henrietta thanked her again and said goodbye.

So, "it's really not unusual," is it? To Henrietta it was very unusual for a member, a talented writer at that, who had joined the club about five years earlier, not to have notified it when he changed his online address, or at the very least, left some explanation on his answering machine. And the club's journal was a comprehensive collection of news from writing groups throughout the state. It was the club's main avenue of communication and way of keeping abreast of each group's activities. To Henrietta's mind, no serious writer would leave town just when it is scheduled to be mailed and not make provision to receive it, unless...

The thought of that "unless" haunted Henrietta all through that evening and persisted into the following morning; by early afternoon, she felt compelled to act.

The jangling phone cut through the usually tranquil peace and quiet of the Southern County sheriff's office, law enforcement center for Dobbsville and its environs. *I knew it couldn't last,* sighed Sheriff Cal Wellesley, as he quelled the disturbance by picking up the receiver. After listening for a moment, the puzzled expression on his face relaxed as he said, "Miss Harcourt? Henrietta? Of course I remember you. It's nice to hear from you. How are you?"

After another moment's silence while he peered at the empty coffee cup on his desk, the puzzled expression returned, this time with deeper furrows. "Yes, yes. I understand. Of course, it's natural to be concerned, although I don't think...," More silence, more furrows. "Yes, all right, well, I'll tell you what I'll do. I'll have one of my men stop in to see Mr. Mercer on his next patrol in that area. Just to make sure everything is all right. Yes, no, that's quite all right. No, no trouble at all; it's what we do. Yes, I'll let you know what we find out; in fact, I'll ask him to call you and reassure you himself. No problem. Glad to help. Thank you, Henrietta. Good-bye."

Sheriff Wellesley slumped into the high-backed, tightly upholstered security of his deluxe model No. 472 Executive Comfort arm chair and reflected on the exchange in which he had just participated. He recalled the event which first caused Miss Henrietta Harcourt to enter his previously ordered existence: He had asked for her. Well, no, not her specifically, just a volunteer to lighten the public traffic at the front counter. Her duties, as he recalled now, were quite specific: simply greet people entering the building and direct them to whatever department or person would most likely resolve their business, whatever it may be.

As he looked back, it seemed to him that the first few days passed quite amiably, with Henrietta quietly querying all who entered the front door, and then capably directing them this way and that, upstairs or down to the lower level of offices. By the second week, however, he became aware that a crush of people began backing up at the reception desk. Well, maybe not so much backing up as gathering around.

When he managed to position himself closely enough to overhear the exchanges between Henrietta and those with police business on their agenda, he discovered the woman was discussing each situation with the party involved. But not only with the party involved, for in overhearing her comments and the resultant explanations—for that's what they usually were—for speeding, drag racing, littering, theft, fighting, various forms of assault, those witnessing the exchanges would offer their own bits of advice or condemnation regarding the aggrieved parties. Such parties would be directed to their destinations, provided they managed to remember what had brought them to the office in the first place.

A private word with Henrietta would usually disperse the logjam—for a while; however, it soon became apparent that Henrietta saw herself as less a directional function once mayhem had been committed, and as more of a deterrent to prevent further actions necessitating such visits in the first place. So if someone came in requesting the location of the traffic court, for instance, or perhaps the schedule for the next meeting of the local DUI prevention group, Henrietta would ferret out the circumstances of the event that precipitated the required attendance in those sessions and, in the course of her initial drawing out of the hapless defendants, others in line, who by then had become spectators to Henrietta's probing questions, offered their own comments—some directed toward the defendants, others to Henrietta herself—and not all were kindly. It certainly became a dilemma. Henrietta was a kind woman who truly only wanted to help everyone she met; in fact, those who had managed to get by her and on to their destinations often came back for advice on new travails that had transpired and over which they were in a quandary.

But eventually enough was enough, and, much as he found the task distasteful, Sheriff Wellesley determined that he had no choice but to request that Henrietta find another outlet for her altruism. He was debating how to approach the matter when Henrietta herself brought about the most satisfactory conclusion. She quit. Oh, she was quite reluctant to do so, she explained, but the fall conference of the writers' group for which she was also registrar was fast approaching, and Henrietta felt she simply could not contend with the volume of anticipated registrations and do justice to her position as receptionist for the law enforcement facility.

Sheriff Wellesley properly expressed dismay at her decision, and assured her they would resign themselves to doing without her as best they could. That's what he told her, and so that's how they parted, with Henrietta blissfully unaware of the subdued elation left in her wake.

* * *

When Deputy Jason Crowley detoured during his daily patrol and turned off the main road, he noted the open mailbox with Matt Mercer's route number, and the several pieces of mail inside waiting to be retrieved. In spite of his extensive background with the Highway Patrol, the sight unnerved him, and he drove slowly along the narrow gravel road as the overgrown shrubbery on either side brushed his cruiser.

At first, he had welcomed the break in his normal routine, the result of a request by his superior that he check the well-being of a local resident. All Deputy Crowley knew was that the man's mail had gone uncollected and, being unable to reach Mr. Mercer, another resident had become concerned and requested a check, resulting in Deputy Crowley's presence on the scene. It wasn't a particularly strange request, although such concern was usually found to be groundless, the result of someone's simple failure to alert a neighbor of a planned absence.

Dismissing his initial unease, Deputy Crowley expected a quick and simple resolution to the matter as he approached a clearing in the dense brush and a cabin came into view. He drove to within twenty feet of the front door, stopped, turned off the engine, and sat for a moment surveying the setting. It was orderly enough, nothing out of sorts that he could see right off hand. A black late model extended cab pickup truck was parked near the front door, and a cord of wood sat tidily stacked against the west wall of the cabin. But no lights shone through the windows, no smoke wafted up from the chimney on this chilly September morning, no dog ran out to challenge an intruder. A small shed was visible beyond the cabin, and an outhouse peeked through the shrubbery a little farther on.

Deputy Crowley didn't like it. Nothing definite that he could put his finger on, but more of a feeling that nagged him; something was wrong. He decided to check in, to alert the dispatcher to his last whereabouts and the condition of the area—just in case.

Instead of bounding from his cruiser as was his habit, always eager to get on with the job at hand, this time he hesitated, instead once more looking around before slowly lifting the door latch and stepping out of the cruiser. He stood beside the vehicle, listening, his eyes scanning the perimeter of the property. Nothing. Instinctively he drew his Glock and held it close to and slightly behind his body as he walked uneasily up the stone path to the front door. He knocked, softly at first, to avoid raising a needless alarm. No sound emanated from inside. Now he knocked louder and called out, "Mr. Mercer? Sheriff's Department. Open the door please." Still nothing. He peered through the bay window beside the door to see if he could make out anything inside. Seeing nothing from the front of the house, he followed the walk to the rear door and squinted through the kitchen window. He could see a table sitting in the middle of the room; a box lay on top, one that looked like it might have contained food. Through the sunlight that flooded the room, he could make out several dead mice on the table beside the box.

Deputy Crowley stepped back and considered the situation. *Should he force his way in? Call for back up? Investigate further?* He once more strained to see what he could through the smeary glass. This time he saw the floor of the kitchen and traced it to a doorway to the next room. There was no mistaking what lay on the floor blocking the way. Two legs were visible up to the knees; they were not moving.

Aware that every move he made now could compromise and even contaminate an investigation, he returned to his cruiser to radio headquarters and report his findings. He was told to secure the scene until the sheriff arrived, whereupon Deputy Crowley holstered his pistol and settled in to wait.

Sheriff Wellesley picked up Doc Rawley, who acted as the county's medical examiner, on the way to the Mercer cabin. Parking beside the black pick-up, the sheriff waited for Crowley to join them, and then the three of them walked to the front door. While the deputy and doctor waited, the sheriff walked around to the rear door to peer through the window; the scene inside was as Deputy Crowley described it.

Returning to the waiting duo at the front of the cabin, he tried the door; finding it locked and seemingly dead bolted, he took a chance and looked for an outside key that might have been hidden as a spare in the event Mercer inadvertently locked himself out. The three of them spent a few minutes examining anything that might serve as a hiding place for an extra key; no luck. Unwilling to bull the door open, they decided to smash out the window in the rear door. Deputy Crowley did the honors while the others looked on. Breaking out the large pane over the locks, he reached in to open the lock and turn back the deadbolt. The door opened easily with a turn of the knob, and the trio entered the tiny cabin.

Each had been prepared for the putrid odor that announced something dead. It wasn't there. Other than a musty smell typical of a cabin needing airing out, there were no other scents to prepare them for what they found once they made their way to the middle of the room. Looking closer at the dead carcasses of the mice that littered the table, Doc Rawley muttered, "Well, I'll be. They're mummified. Dry as dust."

While the doctor paused at the kitchen table, Sheriff Wellesley walked past him to the body in the doorway, the one Crowley had seen from the window. He inspected the body without touching it. Like the mice, the body was desiccated, the skin like tanned leather stretched over a skeletal frame. "You gotta see this, Doc," he called. Then, "Crowley? I want pictures—of everything." Deputy Crowley retreated to the cruiser for his camera.

Returning once again to the rear entrance, the deputy reentered the cabin and proceeded to snap everything as he made his way through the kitchen. A wave of revulsion was squelched as he took numerous photos of the body from different angles, both face down as it was initially found, and then again after Doc Rawley turned it over. Crowley had never seen anything like it, at least not up close like this; the nearest he can describe what he was looking at was pictures he'd seen of archaeological discoveries of people who had died thousands of years ago.

"What do you think, Doc?" the sheriff asked. "Natural causes?"

"Just offhand, I think so. Looks like a stroke or heart attack. With both doors locked from the inside, homicide doesn't seem likely."

"That's my thinking. But when, would you say? How long would it take to cause a condition like this?"

"Hard to say. Heat would have stepped it up some. Depends how long that would have lasted—out here I suppose he heated with propane; we need to know when he last got an order, if it appears the heat was on until the supply ran out. But still, just off the top of my head, I'd say this could happen over two to three months."

"So he's been dead since July, even June?"

"Could be. We'll see what the state lab says. In the meantime, bag everything and take it in—and I mean everything." The doctor aimed this last remark at Crowley, who just nodded.

The sheriff called for an ambulance to transport the body to the county morgue. Deputy Crowley got one of the plastic garbage bags he carried in his supply kit and gathered the empty box and mouse carcasses from the kitchen table. It was one of the few times he wished he were in another line of work.

* * *

Henrietta managed to contain her curiosity for an entire week before the lack of any further communication from either the errant Mr. Mercer or the sheriff's office absolutely forced her to follow up on her previous inquiry. Upon learning of the sheriff's discovery, Henrietta was suitably appalled; to think, a member of her writers' group, a particularly talented author at that, found the way he had been—why, if it hadn't been for her, there's no telling how long the situation might have gone undiscovered, even the sheriff had to admit that, which he did to her satisfaction.

"So, Sheriff, you have, I take it, ruled out any possibility of foul play in the matter of Mr. Mercer's demise?"

"We can't be sure until we get the results of the autopsy, but I would surely be surprised if anything unusual came to light, so I guess you'd say that, right now, yes, we are looking at the death as due to natural causes."

"I see," Henrietta replied thoughtfully. But the truth was that she did not see, not at all. Why had no one questioned his disappearance earlier? The box the sheriff found on the table, which bore the logo of a local bakery—how did it get there? Did Matt bring it in? Did someone else? A friend? Relative? Was it something he had ordered and simply had delivered? And how much of whatever it contained had he consumed before he was stricken? And what could have affected him so suddenly that he was unable to summon help? Was it some long standing condition that suddenly flared up and caused his death?

No, Henrietta decided; there were a number of questions she would need answered before she would accept a verdict of "natural causes."

"Well, thank you, Sheriff," she said. "I guess I can move Mr. Mercer to the Inactive list."

Wellesley chuckled. "Yes, I guess you can, Henrietta. I would say Mr. Mercer is definitely inactive. Permanently so."

"Sheriff, I hope you won't consider me a pest, but I am a writer, you know, and I'm very interested in what's happened here. In fact, the whole premise has potential. Think of it: Mummified remains of reclusive writer found in remote cabin. Local police baffled; investigation planned."

Now Wellesley was laughing out loud. "Now, hold on there, Henrietta. I can go along with all of it except the part about the 'local police baffled.' Not yet, we're not. At this point, there's no mystery except in your imagination. Tell you what—if that changes, you'll be the first to know."

"Thank you, Sheriff. I'll keep in touch."

"Oh, I'm sure you will, Henrietta," the sheriff sighed. "I'm sure you will."

* * *

Bart Hollowell was tired. He had been up since three that morning, as usual, to heat the ovens and finish the frozen ready-to-bake goods that came in from a supplier in Milwaukee. Three a.m. this morning. Three a.m. every morning for the past ten years, all so the bakery could open at six with a suitable assortment of "freshly baked goods." The usual basic breads, doughnuts, pies and cakes came in with slight variations from week to week; only the sweet breads and holiday novelties provided any real change of scene in the showcases that lined the walls of the little shop that so far had provided him with a reasonable livelihood, as long as his needs extended little beyond his mortgage payments and day-to-day living expenses. Ten years of day-in and day-out drudgery, of hoping for a ship to come in that had long since been lost at sea. But now, finally, he looked forward to a better life on the horizon, all courtesy of Uncle Matt. And it had all been so simple. Why hadn't he thought of it sooner?

* * *

Over the next several weeks, Henrietta busied herself with the mundane tasks that made up her world—tending her garden, volunteering at the local library, tending to those necessary details involving the writers' club membership, catching up with her pen pals, and gathering tidbits for the monthly blog she began shortly after her retirement from the Dobbs County health department, where she had been employed as a clerk for the better part of twenty-seven years. Busied physically, that is. Mentally her agile mind continued its preoccupation with the death of Matt Mercer.

But why? Why, she asked herself over and over, couldn't she let it go? Why did the man's death haunt her waking hours? Why was she fixated on what, on the surface, was no more than the natural death of an elderly gentleman who lived alone? Perhaps, she finally acknowledged, it was because of a feeling that had been her constant companion ever since she had retrieved the envelope with those fateful words she could not get out of her mind, "temporarily away," a feeling gnawingly and starkly simple: Something was wrong.

The next day, Henrietta called Sheriff Wellesley. She tried to keep her tone and interest light—that of a budding novelist intrigued with a mysterious death. The sheriff, fortunately, accepted her continued inquiry in his usual good-natured manner, and indulged her questions regarding any possible investigation into Mr. Mercer's demise. His additional input raised her curiosity and suspicion quotient to warning levels. It seems that the routine autopsy revealed an inordinate amount of carbon monoxide in Mr. Mercer's body, so much so in fact, that Dr. Rawley felt it could not have been a one-time occurrence. In other words, Matt had been poisoned by the deadly emissions for a considerable length of time prior to the massive stroke that eventually killed him.

Now Henrietta was aghast. How could that be, she inquired? Surely the man would have known if there had been a malfunction in his utility line. Gas smelled, didn't it? With a distinct odor purposely added to the liquid propane to warn of such possible leakage? Matt was not a stupid man; how could he not have been aware of an ongoing seepage of poisonous gas?

"It happens, Henrietta; fortunately not often, but the danger is always there, and sometimes it just sneaks through; don't forget—it _is_ called a silent killer. It's not just silent, it's also insidious, and in this case, it appears there may have been factors present that masked the odor long enough for the poison to accumulate in Mercer's system and trigger the stroke that killed him. It's rare, but it's been known to happen," the sheriff assured her.

"Factors that masked the telltale odor? Sheriff, carbon monoxide has been described as smelling like anything from, on the mild side, rotten eggs, to other things that are not mentioned in polite company. How could it have happened?"

"Well, the outside tank was pretty rusty inside; that'll do it. Then too, Mercer was a smoker; we found a number of pipes and several varieties of loose tobacco laying about his house. That kind of smoke will go a long way in covering up another odor, and don't forget the way a gas leak works—it would have affected his judgment, his perception, to the point that he may not have realized anything was wrong; then, in the end, he could have become simply too disoriented to call for help. It's a tragedy, Henrietta, that's all I can say."

"That it is, Sheriff," she agreed, "that it is. But tell me, didn't Matt have any visitors who might have noticed something wrong even if he couldn't? Surely there must have been someone—a friend, relative, neighbor—who would have noticed when he wasn't seen about as usual?"

"Well, he has a nephew. Bart Hollowell, his brother's son, owns a small bakery in Pleasant Corners. Being in the same town and all, I imagine they have a relationship, but I can't rightly say just how close they are. Far as I know, Bart's the only kin."

"I see," Henrietta said softly, more to herself than the sheriff. Then, "Sheriff, would you happen to know if Matt had a will? Would you say he was a wealthy man at all?"

"Henrietta, I imagine he was wealthy compared to most people in these parts. This county has the highest unemployment rate in the state; it doubled overnight when that auto parts plant pulled out a few years ago. Most everyone who could get to it worked there, in some cases whole families were on the payroll. It hit a lot of folks hard when it closed, that's for sure."

"Well, Sheriff, I appreciate your taking the time to talk to me. You've been very kind. I won't take up any more of your time, but I hope I can call you again? I'd like to bounce some ideas off you to make sure my story is plausible."

"Any time, Henrietta. Glad to help if I can," the sheriff assured her amiably.

After they hung up, Henrietta sat awhile ruminating on their conversation. Before long, she determined that a visit to Pleasant Corners was definitely in order.

* * *

It had been a productive day, Henrietta thought later with a modicum of satisfaction as she sat in her driveway watching the door of her garage slowly rise until it was high enough to clear her car. She slowly drove forward and stopped in the middle of the spacious interior, mentally reviewing the day's activity before swinging the doors wide and making her exit.

It had been an easy hour's drive to the beauty salon in Pleasant Corners, and her appointment for a wash and set was honored promptly; she had arranged for an additional manicure in the event extra time might be beneficial. During these ministrations, she had engaged her operator in small talk, eventually approaching the topic in which she was most interested, and in actuality the purpose of her visit—Bart Hollowell—and in that regard, her time had been well spent. Bart was well known and the subject of occasional conversation among the clientele of the salon, and Henrietta's operator felt no compunction in relating whatever tidbits of information concerning him that came to mind.

According to local knowledge, Bart Hollowell had spent a good deal of his early life simply knocking about, subsisting on whatever odd jobs he could find, and had acquired a reputation as a reasonably competent jack-of-all-trades handyman. About ten years ago, he wrangled enough money, some say from his uncle, to buy out a local bakery that had gone into foreclosure. Although the place provided a passable income, financially he lived on the edge, occupying quarters above the shop, spending what he made week by week. His principal methods of transportation were a light blue panel truck with rusted fenders which he used for deliveries and supplies, and a vintage Harley

Softail which apparently required constant tinkering, an activity that consumed the majority of Bart's free time.

That he was Matt Mercer's nephew was well known. Also well known was the amount of attention Bart lavished on his Uncle Matt of late, attention that had been mostly non-existent until about six months ago, when his cycle, with its ear shattering exhaust and trail of blue smoke, suddenly began frequenting the highway turnoff to Matt's woodsy retreat.

Little was known of Matt Mercer, the prototype of the reclusive writer, other than gossip gleaned from tidbits of information regarding his limited interaction with the inhabitants of the tiny township. Because of this, much was made of his frequent and generous contributions to any worthwhile cause concerning the town's residents or improvement projects. It was rumored that Matt had been a shrewd investor who now was able to live quite well off the interest on various funds to which he had contributed since he was old enough to hold a paying job.

Gathering this background material had taken all of the hair set and part of the manicure, although Henrietta did not think a return trip for either would be necessary. She had learned enough.

* * *

Sheriff Wellesley returned from a late lunch and settled into a review of the warrants that had arrived in the day's mail when his phone rang. Alerted that Henrietta Harcourt was asking to speak with him, the sheriff took a moment to recall their previous conversation before he picked up the receiver.

"Miss Harcourt," he said graciously, "how nice to hear from you. How's your story coming?"

"That's what I'm calling about, Sheriff. I have a beginning premise I'd like to discuss with you, if you have the time," Henrietta replied.

Welcoming a break from the violent notices before him, Wellesley said, "Absolutely. What do you have?"

Henrietta proceeded to describe the substance of her latest mystery. It concerned a hermit living in a rural area who was discovered dead after an accumulation of mail alerted authorities and prompted an investigation. *In the story,* the hermit was murdered by a ne'er-do-well nephew who tampered with his propane gas lines under the guise of a routine installation of a new space heater. *In the story,* the nephew arouses suspicion due to recent uncharacteristically solicitous visits to the old man after previously ignoring their relationship. The clincher: the nephew's visits stopped as abruptly as they had started, at about the time the coroner set the approximate time of death. *In the story,* had the visits continued, the death would have been discovered earlier, but they stopped in order to allow the tampered pipes to oxidize in an attempt to obliterate the marks made by the wrench in loosening the connection.

"Well, Sheriff, what do you think?" Henrietta queried innocently.

The line was silent for several minutes. Henrietta began to wonder if they had been disconnected when the sheriff finally replied.

"Miss Harcourt," he said coolly, "this seems eerily similar to the situation with Matt Mercer. Are you sure this is just a bit of poetic license, or are you implying something, which, if I were you, I wouldn't do without a good deal of solid evidence, which, at the present time, doesn't exist to my knowledge."

"Well, Sheriff, I did say the situation lent itself to a delicious mystery. I simply fleshed out the "what ifs" to suggest how it could have been done, if, of course, that had been what actually happened in real life."

"All right, Henrietta, I'll go along with this premise; but I'd naturally be very interested in learning the basis for the conclusion that the nephew did it."

"Of course, you do understand, Sheriff," Henrietta continued blithely, "that the usual caveat applies, the one about all characters and situations being entirely fictional and any similarity to anyone living or dead being purely coincidental."

"I understand, Henrietta. Please continue. I'd like to know how your fictional sleuth solves this fictional situation."

"Gossip, Sheriff—follow the gossip and confirm the inferences."

"Such as?"

"Well, now, Sheriff, you understand, of course, that this is all just supposition—an exploration of the premise underlying a fictional account of the motive for a fictional murder."

"Yes, Henrietta. I understand we're just supposing here, but I'd still be interested in your fictional sleuth's train of thought. Tell me about it."

"All right, then, here's what I have so far: In this story, my protagonist is a law officer in a rural community, much as yourself, actually; but, for the sake of reference, let's say he's a deputy sheriff. Anyway, a local resident is found dead in much the same circumstances as Mr. Mercer. On the surface, it all appears to be a tragic accident.

"But something nags at my hero—I haven't settled on a name at this point. Well, as I said, something just doesn't set right, so he begins to nose around, just casually asking questions about the dead man's habits, gathering information on his friends, family, and in particular, whoever may have visited him in the weeks or months before he died.

"Since the location is a rural setting, and since the surrounding houses are occupied by either housewives or retired people, in other words, people who would likely be home a good deal of the time and in a position to notice traffic in and out of the only road leading to the dead man's cabin, our hero interviews those residents. He learns that the dead man was very much a recluse, although everyone knew him to be a writer whose work had appeared in various outdoor magazines, as well as the local paper, from time to time in articles on conservation.

"Now then, these casual conversations uncover information that lead the deputy to look at the man's nephew, not initially as a suspect, you understand, but again in the guise of casual investigation. Now this nephew, a bit of a jack-of-all-trades in the area, was known to be unable to ever hold on to his money, yet several months before his uncle's death, he began running up his charge cards, as if he expected to shortly receive a windfall that would cover his debts. It was in this period that our deputy learns of a series of visits to the uncle's cabin, visits that had been non-existent prior to this time, visits that stopped as abruptly as they began.

"A bit more nosing around uncovers that the nephew had recently purchased a gas space heater which was charged to his uncle's account, while making a point of mentioning that his uncle intended to install the unit himself.

"At this point, there is nothing untoward in the man's actions, until the deputy learns that the uncle suffered from cataracts—to the point that his vision was impaired and he had so far delayed the operation that would allow him to resume his writing activities. It was not hard to uncover this information; all it took was a few phone calls to the man's publishers. It seems the dead man's eyesight had grown progressively worse in the past year and he knew he would soon have to undergo the removal of the cataracts, but he dreaded the procedure and wanted to forego the event as long as possible; that time, however, was getting nearer and his activities were becoming more and more limited.

"The point of all this is a theory that it was the nephew, not his uncle, who installed the propane space heater, and who, in the course of the installation, failed to tighten the connections sufficiently to avoid a gas leak. In addition, there was never a call for an inspection of the installation, as the law requires, as a safety measure in preventing exactly the kind of gas leak that caused the uncle's death. The slow leak eventually did its work when the weather turned chilly and the closed windows and doors prevented any fresh air from diluting the leaking gas. Being a smoker, the uncle didn't notice the slight odor that signaled a leaking gas line. As the gas accumulated, it affected his judgment and clouded his memory, until the carbon monoxide caused him to pass out; at that point, the gas slowly replaced the oxygen in his blood and caused his death. Once this occurred, the nephew simply sat back and waited until the inevitable happened: the body was discovered, as he knew it would be eventually, and he was notified of the tragedy.

"Being the only relative, the nephew was sure he would be the beneficiary of the life insurance policy he knew his uncle kept in a safe deposit box—he'd seen it once. Also, he planned on selling the cabin and the surrounding acreage, probably for a pretty penny as a recreational or private hunting parcel to someone from the Twin Cities, little more than an hour away."

Henrietta paused. "Well, Sheriff, that's what I've got so far. How does it sound? Do you think it's possible? Do you think this is how a killer might operate, in the story?"

In the silence that followed, Henrietta wondered if the sheriff were still on the line, or if he had quietly laid the receiver down and gone off, leaving her to prattle on at length.

"Sheriff?" she ventured. "Are you there?"

She was beginning to be concerned. What could be going on? Was he still on the line? Was he angry at her fictional account of a scenario that so closely mimicked a very real occurrence? Had she hit too close to home?

Finally she heard a deep breath, and then he said, "Yes, Henrietta. I'm here," he said quietly. "And I don't appreciate what I've just heard. I warn you again that this had better indeed be nothing more than a figment of your imagination, because I'm telling you, you are dangerously close to slandering Bart Hollowell."

"That certainly is not my intention, Sheriff," Henrietta said calmly. "My story is pure fiction, propelled only, and very loosely, by the circumstances of Mr. Mercer's demise. Think of it: the mummified remains of a reclusive writer discovered in a rural cabin, a discovery prompted simply by his failure to renew his membership in a writers' organization in which he had long been a member. It really is just too good not to stir the imagination of anyone who even remotely purports to be a serious writer."

"Maybe," the sheriff reluctantly and very tentatively agreed, "but it just sounds a mite too close for comfort to me. I only hope you've covered your tracks as far as the location and individuals involved here, or you could find yourself on the serious end of a lawsuit."

"Not to worry, Sheriff. Any identification to either will be labeled purely circumstantial; and, after all, it is, of course."

The sheriff's silence said it all—he didn't believe her.

* * *

The sheriff couldn't shake his unease over Henrietta's call and the basic premise of her story. He told himself the woman was just a busybody, amusing herself with fictional accounts of incidents devoid of any truthful content. But his own truth was even more unsettling, for the woman's supposedly fictional scenario hit eerily close to actual plausibility, and that presented him with a conundrum: Because she, or rather, her fictional account, presented the possibility of an actual occurrence, did he have a responsibility to investigate her fictional innuendoes to see how closely they mirrored real life? He wondered, and the possibility bothered him, feeding a suspicion that nagged him relentlessly in the following days, try as he may to put both Henrietta and her fictional sleuth out of his mind. He was successful for two entire days, and then he called Deputy Crowley into his office.

"Mornin', Sheriff," Crowley said. "You wanted to see me?"

"Yes, Jason. Sit down. Get yourself some coffee if you want," the sheriff said, motioning the pot behind him; the freshly brewed aroma wafted toward them.

"Thanks, believe I will." The deputy helped himself to a paper cup from the stack beside the pot and filled it three quarters full with coffee, being sure to leave room for the half and half the sheriff preferred in place of the powdered creamer available in the lounge, and which he purchased himself and kept several small cartons of in the little bar refrigerator that stood next to his credenza.

Sheriff Wellesley waited for his deputy to return to his seat and watched him place the steaming brew on the desk within his reach, before he said, "I've been thinking about the Matt Mercer thing."

"Oh? What about it? The doc said natural causes, so case closed—no?" Deputy Crowley had never been one to look for trouble, and he felt a sudden and definite twinge of unease that the matter he saw as a slam dunk death was being brought up.

"Maybe no," the sheriff said thoughtfully. "It just seems a bit too tidy. Could be there's nothing more to it than what it seems, but also could be that maybe we should take another look at that cabin; and maybe ask a few questions. Like who would benefit from Mercer's death, and if that party might have benefited enough to have maybe helped it along."

Oh, man...no...don't tell me he's going to make a federal case out of it just because an old codger croaked, Crowley thought; but he just said, "Well, of course, if you think there's something not quite right, yeah, well, sure, we should check it out."

"Glad you feel that way," the sheriff said, knowing full well the deputy's reluctance to do any more than the minimum he could get away with. "You get a contractor and go over the house, especially the gas connections. See if anything new was installed; if not, check the old connections; see if it all looks like it should, whatever that is. I'm going to talk to the neighbors and Bart Hollowell; might run over to the county seat, too, and nose around the record office."

"Okay, Sheriff. I'll get right on it." The deputy drained his cup and headed for the door, fully intending to make a quick call to one of the local heating contractors to look things over; a quick all clear and he could go back to cruising the county.

With Crowley out of the way, Sheriff Wellesley set about planning his own course of action. It was early enough in the day for a drive out to Mercer's neighborhood; then he'd see what he could find out.

The sun was up, the traffic was down, and the temperature flirted with seventy as the sheriff pulled into the driveway of Mercer's nearest neighbor, Jack Puchek, maybe an eighth of a mile up the road from Mercer's cabin. He was Mercer's nearest neighbor, and the sheriff hoped the two had been neighborly enough to provide at least a little information on the reclusive writer's recent activities. Jack was a retired miner who didn't get out much anymore since arthritis stiffened him up so it was too painful for much more than watching the woods from his picture window, which fortunately faced Mercer's place.

Jack welcomed the sheriff, grateful for company of any kind, and fixed them up with some coffee and yesterday's donuts. A few pleasantries and Sheriff Wellesley got to the point. "Mr. Puchek, I'm sure by now you probably heard what happened to Matt Mercer. So far it looks like a pure accident, but I'd like to get a little more information before I close the case on this one. Anything you can tell me?"

Puchek debated just what, and how much, to let on what he knew and how much he suspected. He had to be careful, or his neighbor's accident could be catching. "About what, Sheriff? And what makes you think I know anything at all? I don't spy on nobody."

Wellesley smiled and said quietly, "Not sayin' you do, Mr. Puchek. But there's not much you could miss from your front window there; sure must give you a fine view of Matt's place. All I want to know is whether you two talked at all or if you saw anything that seemed out of the way recently." Then he added, "Do you think it was anything more than an accident? Maybe a reason to think so?"

Puchek hesitated. He drank his coffee, stirred it with his spoon, and took his time with his donut. Finally, the sheriff said, "There is something, isn't there, Mr. Puchek? I'd appreciate anything you'd care to pass along; maybe it has nothing to do with what happened, but we'll never know if you don't say something."

"It probably don't mean nothin', but I just thought it kind of funny how much that nephew of Matt's seemed to be paying him quite a bit of attention for a spell, seein' how he hadn't bothered much before during the twenty or so years Matt lived next door. Matt was over one day about three, maybe four months ago when he wanted to use my phone to order some fuel. Seems like that last storm knocked his phone out. Anyway, we got to talkin', and he mentioned how Bart was his only kin now and how sorry he was that they wasn't close. Said he called Bart from time to time just to keep in touch, but Bart didn't seem to have no time for him. Then, about maybe a few months ago, it suddenly seemed like Bart couldn't stay away. If it wasn't his Harley, it was that truck of his rattling up the drive two, three times a week; then they stopped, just as sudden. Jus' seemed funny, that's all I'm sayin'."

"I see," the sheriff said slowly. "Any idea what caused the activity?"

"No, Sheriff, not a one. But one day I did see him haulin' something out of the back of that blue van of his. A big box. Well, I admit I was curious, so I took a look with my binoculars, the one I use watchin' the birds, you know, an' it said somethin' like Heat Rite hot water tank. I know they sell those up at Albert's hardware in town. So I figured Matt had asked Bart to pick up a tank for him, that's all. Wondered who'd install it though. Happen to know Matt had cataracts so bad he told me he could hardly see at all, but didn't want to go to the doctor, 'cause she's told him for years they needed to come off, but he just didn't want to go in. Said he'd have to, though, cause things were closin' down on him; he'd had to quit his writin', and that was goin' real hard on him; he missed workin' on his stories, I know that for sure. Anyway, he said he'd have to just make up his mind to go and get it done, and I'm sure he was fixin' to do that when I heard about him bein' found like that. Awful, that's what it was, plumb awful."

The sheriff looked at the old man and considered what he'd just heard. He had a feeling Puchek had wanted to tell someone about it for some time, but would not have come forward on his own. Now that he'd gotten it off his chest, Wellesley doubted he would get any more out of him.

"Well, thank you, Mr. Puchek. That was real interesting. Nothing wrong with folks visitin' one another, that's for sure."

"That's what I thought, Sheriff. Nothin' wrong at all."

Wellesley finished his coffee and asked if Puchek needed anything, seeing how he'd lost his closest neighbor; he said he'd send his deputy over from time to time to check on him. Puchek said he was fine, but would appreciate Crowley coming over; Jason used to join them when his dad and Puchek went squirrel hunting; he wondered if Jason still went. Wellesley said he didn't know.

* * *

Bart Hollowell studied the glossy brochure in his hands, the one he'd picked it up along with several others from the Harley dealer in Pleasant Corners; the salesman had been real cooperative, asking Bart just what he had in mind, and suggesting several models, any of which would be just the thing for the kind of road trips Bart had in mind.

The model he had pretty much settled on was the 1200 Low Sportster with an air-cooled engine and electronic fuel injection system. The bike was loaded with an array of electronic gadgets that did all but talk; in their own way, he guessed they did that too. The one detail that he spent more time on than any other was the color. Single color black, blue, or red; or two-tone variations of the single colors? It wasn't their top-of-the-line model, for sure, but just one of the uses he had decided to indulge when Uncle Matt's money came through.

And he never doubted it would come through; he just wasn't sure when or how much he could expect; but whatever cash or stocks or whatever else the old man had was part of the legacy he expected;

there was also the cabin and the five acres of prime land bordering the national forest on which it was located. He had already decided he would get a realtor from the Twin Cities to handle it as a private getaway for some well-heeled city slickers; that's where the money was, he had decided, not with locals who saw it as nothing more than scrub land that should go for a song.

He was finding it plumb difficult to wait, he knew that much. Since the parts plant closed, his business about closed with it. He was running on fumes and didn't know how much longer he could hold on. He wanted to sell, but who would take the place off his hands, knowing they wouldn't be able to make a go of it any more than he had? It was no good as commercial property, that much he was sure of.

While Bart had managed to be patient so far, he was beginning to get itchy. The man from the Harley store had called several times, pestering him for a decision on the new models he'd checked out last week. Still, he didn't want to appear too eager; it might look funny. The attorney who was acting as Uncle Matt's executor had been sidelined for a while with some unexpected surgery and was home recuperating; his secretary said it would be another week or so, but he would surely be in touch as soon as he could to settle up. Then Bart could get on with the plans he'd been working on ever since he decided that Uncle Matt was good for a real windfall, what with the money he'd made from his books, photographs, and articles over the years; not to mention his cabin, where he'd lived like a pauper for the last twenty-some years.

The lawyer had called him as soon as he had been notified by the bank of Uncle Matt's death; said then he would be in touch as soon as he had a chance to review Uncle Matt's wishes; then his appendix acted up and he had to go into the hospital.

Uncle Matt had assured Bart many times that, as his only living relative, it would all be his. He had never been able to pin the old man down on an amount, and had never actually seen his will; in fact, was surprised to learn he had one; didn't know what he needed one for, with only one relative to leave things too; didn't seem all that complicated to Bart.

But Uncle Matt had said whenever the subject came up that he wanted to be sure Bart got what he had coming. No, there had to be money there, all right; lots of money; and soon it would all be his. And it had all been so simple—that's the beauty of easy money. Once he had decided on the method, the execution kind of took care of itself. Granted, he had expected, really hoped for, an explosion, rather than the old man keeling over from the fumes and not being found for weeks. But Bart figured dead was dead whichever way it happened; he wasn't fussy.

* * *

Instead of a local heating contractor, it was the inspector from the state licensing bureau who met Deputy Crowley at Mercer's cabin early afternoon that Friday. Crowley sat in his cruiser while the man disappeared first into the cabin and then into the crawl space underneath to check the gas lines. He had been more than a bit concerned when he found out that no request for inspection had been made after the installation of the water heater. In fact, he had been reluctant to approach the cabin at all until he had been assured the tanks had been empty for weeks and the cabin had been thoroughly aired out after the body had been discovered and removed. Seemed to Crowley the man took a long time just to run a flashlight over some pipes, and passed the time with a Grisham novel he'd just started. Crowley was beginning the third chapter when the inspector emerged from the boarded up opening beneath the building's foundation, checked to see that the front door to the cabin was locked, and walked slowly toward the cruiser. He opened the passenger door and slid in beside Crowley. The two spoke for several minutes, and then agreed to meet back in the sheriff's office as soon as they could get there.

* * *

Charlie Cooke was feeling particularly pleased with himself as he cruised the Interstate toward the turnoff at 45 in Pleasant Corners. He was just coming off his first run with his new truck, and all had gone well. The extended-hood sleeper cab's ten aluminum wheels skimmed along under the 425 hp engine, with its smoothly integrated fifteen speed transmission.

It was ten years old and had cost him dearly, that's for sure, but the truck and the reinvention it promised after his twenty years on the parts plant's assembly line were worth it, he told himself. As far as he was concerned, the truck was a honey, and he was now a licensed independent long-haul trucker who had spent this first run hauling a refrigerated produce trailer to a major market chain in Chicago. He hadn't gotten a return load on this trip, but that would come, he told himself, as he became better known among the trucking agencies he contracted with.

This trip had been kind of a shakedown cruise, anyway, as Charlie checked out the tilt steering wheel, the backup sensor system, the CD player, and especially the CB radio, which he was still trying to get the hang of. But it was a dandy, with forty channels, seven for weather alone; and after dark it lit up in the dash real good. He had tried it out at his first stop on I-90 moving toward Chi Town and hooked up with a couple of veteran drivers who called themselves Hangdog and Choo Choo.

The three had arranged to meet for breakfast that first morning at Louie's Eat 'N Go in the Four Corners truck stop. Charlie liked his new friends and the CB handle they gave him—Charlie Brown.

Once back on the road, the three kept up a spirited banter that caused the miles to disappear, even if Charlie was a little slow at picking up the lingo the other two spewed out effortlessly. But he soon found himself automatically slowing down when either of them mentioned bear traps, getting cut off by a big R, or getting their doors blown off by a bulldog. When they first talked about an alligator in the road, he thought they meant an escapee from a reptile farm, until they clued him that it meant a blown tire in the road.

Charlie found the microphone a bit cumbersome, big and a little hard to handle, but he was getting used to it; if he weren't as easy with it as his new friends, well, he would just keep that to himself.

* * *

After conferring with his deputy and the inspector from the state licensing agency, Sheriff Wellesley made a couple of phone calls. Then, figuring it was time for a face-to-face with Bart Hollowell, he drove out to Bart's Bakery in the strip mall on Old State 45.

The mall itself wasn't much anymore, with mostly vacant and shuttered store fronts scattered among the few die-hard businesses still operating, mainly a Laundromat, a CPA service, a pizzeria, and the bakery. It had once been a vibrant community center, home to three restaurants, a twelve-lane bowling alley, and a small movie theater featuring second run films. But that was in the town's heyday, when the parts plant was running ten- and twelve-hour shifts and traffic flowed off the Interstate at a steady pace with supply trucks and employees from surrounding communities, attracted by the good pay and benefits that employment at the plant provided. It was all gone now. The stoplight regulating traffic off the Interstate had long ago been replaced by a simple stop sign which, after the plant pulled out, was regularly punctuated with BB pellets.

The enticing aroma of freshly baked goods engulfed Wellesley as soon as he entered the single store front beneath Bart's living quarters. His mouth began to water involuntarily, and he wondered how it was living with those smells, for surely they permeated the building and lingered on those off hours when the bakery itself was closed. He swallowed and figured there were surely worse things.

The small shop was neat and inviting; its showcases were old, but clean. A Harley catalog lay next to the register; the sparkling red roadster on the cover about jumped off the page against the dull marble countertop.

Bart was just finishing an order for a dozen hot cross buns for a waiting customer. When the customer had departed, and only the two of them remained in the front section of the store, Sheriff Wellesley asked Bart for a few minutes of his time to answer some questions.

"Sure thing, Sheriff. Just one minute, and I'll be right with you."

Figuring he pretty much knew what those questions were about, Bart went to the front door and flipped the "Come in, we're open." sign to its "Sorry, we're closed." side. After putting a tray of the week's special—cinnamon chocolate chip muffins—into the oven and setting the timer for forty-five minutes, he turned to face his visitor. "All right, Sheriff, what can I do for you?"

"Mister Hollowell, it's about your uncle, Matt Mercer. We've been looking into the death, and come across a couple of puzzling items we'd like to clear up."

"Such as? I thought it was pretty much cut and dried. I don't know all the details, but I understand he had some kind of stroke or heart attack. I got a call from his attorney a while back. He told me he was my uncle's executor and would be getting back to me once he had a chance to review the will. Surprised the hell out of me, I can tell you. Didn't know old Matt even had a will; didn't know he was much for legal stuff. Never said anything to me, that's for sure. But then, we weren't close—never had been."

The sheriff watched Hollowell as he spoke. He was bigger and tougher looking than the sheriff had expected, and Wellesley found it somewhat improbable that during their recent spate of closeness, Bart had not questioned his uncle on his legal preparations; as Mercer's only relation, Wellesley thought it curious that Bart had not asked the old man if there was anything he needed to do if something happened.

It was equally curious that Mercer would not have discussed the disposition of his property with his only kin, especially in light of his increasing disability. Curious indeed. But then, Wellesley thought, perhaps the old man had indeed discussed his will with his nephew, just not telling him the entire truth about his instructions to his executor. It seemed to Wellesley that Bart should have realized the situation from the fact that an attorney, and not Mercer's only kin, was executor; but maybe not.

Roused from his musing, the sheriff began, "Mr. Hollowell, there was a good deal of carbon monoxide discovered in your uncle's tissues. We suspect it had been from some kind of leak in a pipe from the propane tank outside, and probably went on for some time before Mr. Mercer was overcome; that's when we think the stroke occurred, while he was unconscious from the fumes. I just want to know if you noticed anything when you were out there after you bought that water heater for him."

Bart's face remained expressionless, but his eyes bore into the sheriff's, as if trying to fathom what the lawman was really getting at. Then, as if deciding on his story, he replied, "No, Sheriff. Can't say that I did. You see, the thing is, Matt asked me to pick up the tank for him to save the delivery charge. Said he'd install the thing himself. I offered to do it for him, but he insisted he could handle it, so I didn't push."

"I see," the sheriff murmured, considering Bart's reply. Then he said, "You see, Mr. Hollowell, I just had an inspector from the state licensing agency out there to check the connections. He tells me the pipes inside the house weren't as tight as they might have been, and weren't sealed like they should have been. There was no call for inspection, either, which is too bad; it might have uncovered the problem and prevented what happened."

"You're probably right, Sheriff," Bart said, "but, like I told you, he wanted to install the thing himself. I don't know if he did that, or broke down and had someone else take care of it, but I just delivered the tank."

The sheriff considered Hollowell's story. He didn't believe it, but wondered what he could do. Even if Bart admitted to installing the tank, no one could prove he left the pipes loose and unsealed deliberately. With a layman's limited experience, he could claim he did the best he could, thought the connection was secure, and never intended to harm the old man. All the sheriff had was circumstantial evidence, flimsy at that, and he knew it. Still, he played the only card he was sure of.

"I see," the sheriff said again. Then he added, "As long as I'm here, I thought you might like to know I talked to the attorney who is acting as your uncle's executor. Did you know your uncle left a sizeable amount of cash, along with some bonds and other securities? Then, of course, there's his land and the cabin; that'll bring a pretty penny for sure." He stopped at this point to gauge the impact of the information.

Hollowell's face softened into a smile. "That's good to know, Sheriff. Thanks for passing it along."

"Yes, your uncle lived simply, that's for sure," the sheriff continued. "It seems his only outlet was the wolf sanctuary over in Henley, just off 25. His stories about the animals there won a number of awards and publication in several of the major outdoor magazines. Anyway, I suppose you knew your uncle directed his land to be sold and, along with the rest of his assets, the proceeds be put into a trust to help maintain the sanctuary. I'm sure the animals appreciated his friendship while he was alive and his generosity now that he's passed."

The color had drained from Hollowell's face. He stared at the sheriff as if not understanding, or even hearing, what he had just been told. "No," he managed to whisper, "I didn't know."

"Well, I guess it'll all be settled right quick now. Just thought you'd like to know. Thank you for your time, Mr. Hollowell. Take care, now." With that, the sheriff made his way past the showcases lining the aisle to the front door, past the register with its gleaming Harley brochure, and left the shop.

* * *

Henrietta was paging through the sale catalog from her favorite garden supply center. She was trying to decide on a late planting of coneflowers or vibrant asters when the phone rang and she found Sheriff Wellesley on the line.

"Hello, Henrietta. I just thought I'd let you know how our case of the mummified author turned out. But I'm afraid it's not as exciting as the ending your detective will have to come up with to satisfy your readers."

"Oh? And just what was your conclusion regarding Mr. Mercer?"

Wellesley related the outcome of his further investigation and his final conversation with Bart Hollowell.

"So there's nothing more to be done?" she asked.

"I'm afraid not, Henrietta. There's no concrete proof, nothing that he couldn't explain, and whatever charges we might make stick would probably result in no more than probation."

"I see. Well, I'm sure you're right," Henrietta said. "But you know, Sheriff," she continued thoughtfully, "retribution often exists beyond the puny bounds of our judicial system, and somehow I believe Mr. Hollowell will find that out. I don't believe for a minute that he has really escaped punishment."

"No, Henrietta," the sheriff agreed, "I don't believe he has."

* * *

Bart Hollowell remained motionless for several minutes after the sheriff's departure. His head was ringing. He couldn't think. He could barely breathe.

It couldn't be true. It couldn't be. The old man had to know what that money meant to him.

Then suddenly the awful truth struck him like a sucker punch alongside his head. The old man *did* know. He knew all along and had just strung him along, going on and on about Bart being his only kin, and everything being his, and getting everything he had coming.

"...getting everything he had coming." The phrase rang in Bart's head like the reverberation of a gigantic gong. That's what his uncle had told him more than once. Now Bart knew exactly what the old man meant, and his rage was a fearsome thing. He wanted to kill someone. *But, then, he already had.*

Barely aware of his movements, Bart left the shop and mounted his cycle, revving it up, listening to the distinct, thunderous roar of the powerful Harley engine. He released the clutch and the quarter-ton machine roared out the driveway. The cycle wobbled when he turned too sharply on entering the highway. He instinctively let up on the gas to steady it, attempting to steer out of the path of the oncoming traffic, when he saw the emblem on the grill of the truck bearing down on him.

* * *

Charlie Brown and Hangdog had been going around about the upcoming Bears' game and its expected outcome. Charlie hadn't noticed his speed climbing past 70, 75, 80...he was pushing 90 when he veered off the Interstate at the 45 off ramp and dropped his mike. Hangdog's voice was droning on about the game and something about a chicken coop as Charlie fumbled for the mike, glancing down for what he would swear at the inquest was no more than a split second.

But it was enough. When his eyes found the road again, the cycle was coming up fast, the rider square in his path. Panic and instinct collided as Charlie stomped hard on the brakes and viciously punched the horn. But he had twenty tons under him that propelled him forward with shattering momentum. He jerked the wheel. Too late. He heard himself scream when the cab hit the cycle, tumbled over, and skidded into the culvert beside the road.

Charlie was held tight by his safety belt and harness even as the cab rolled; when it finally stopped moving, he was still in his seat, although dazed and barely conscious. Air bags, activated on impact, filled the compartment. A breeze swept over him, carrying the faint smell of burning rubber. He couldn't move; he tried. He didn't feel anything, either; nothing at all. In his foggy confusion, he wondered if he could be dead.

* * *

Willie Eckert had been on duty for twenty-two hours straight and was hoping to coast the remaining two hours of his shift. His hopes evaporated when he heard the radio crackle and the dispatcher's voice drone on about a wreck off the frontage road.

A few miles more and it would have been out of our jurisdiction, Willie thought irritably, even as he scrambled to join the other members of the volunteer ambulance service which operated out of the town hall garage in Haverly Township.

Proud of their recent county-wide award for quickest response time among the neighboring communities that also depended on volunteer EMT responders, Willie joined Eddie Wickers and Marv Chunsky as they took their places in the town's only ambulance.

Eddie and Marv were up front, and the vehicle had already begun to move, when Willie scrambled through the back door into the well-equipped and efficiently-appointed rear compartment. Eddie, taking his turn behind the wheel, hit the siren as they hurried out of the garage, barely clearing the still-rising overhead door. Willie braced himself as he listened to Dispatch brief them with what little was known of the accident.

A passing trucker had seen the rig flip and hurriedly called in a report. A deputy sheriff on routine patrol was alerted by Dispatch and sped to the scene via a little-used back road, pulling up just as a second cruiser arrived. After a hurried discussion between the two, the first deputy proceeded to direct the rescue efforts of the other truckers and motorists who by now had stopped to help. Flares were set to warn oncoming traffic and close the exit ramp; fire extinguishers and box cutters were brought out. The smell of burning rubber and the heat generated by friction when the rig slid into the ditch raised the risk of possible explosion.

The second officer ran to the cycle to assess the situation, almost immediately calling out, "This one's gone." He then went to the truck, climbed on top of the cab, and got the door open just as the ambulance lurched to a halt on the frontage road beside the overturned rig, its siren fading to silence. Willie jumped out the rear door and was the first of the team to reach the rig; Marv was close behind. Eddie turned the ambulance around to return via the secondary highway they had used to reach the scene.

Seeing Willie glance at the mangled cycle, the deputy bracing the door called out, "Never mind that one—no use. Maybe a chance here. Let's get him out!"

After a cursory examination of the driver's condition, Willie and Marv pulled the semi-conscious man from the cab and stabilized him on a backboard for transport.

Charlie, drifting in and out of consciousness, his breathing labored, had felt his rescuers' hands when they deftly cut through his safety belt and harness, pulled at him, lifted him, and when he was moving, floating it seemed. He wondered if he might be dreaming and struggled to open his eyes, but he couldn't.

With their passenger receiving oxygen in the rear of the ambulance, the crew sped to the county hospital fifteen miles away. Willie took Charlie's vital signs and called them out to Marv, who relayed them to the emergency physician on duty at the hospital.

Their passenger would make it, Willie knew that much; but even as he routinely tended his duties, he checked his watch and thought of the next run they would likely make that day—returning to the accident scene to collect the mangled body pinned under the motorcycle. There would be no hurry on that trip, he thought; he might still coast out on the last run of his shift.

Back in the empty bakery, the eerie silence was broken by the clear sharp ping of the oven timer—This Week's Special was ready.

- The End –

- Call To Duty -

The old Chevy rumbled to life as soon as Rick turned the key. As usual, the radio was on and tuned to his favorite station of top ten hits; the system's four custom speakers blared loudly enough to announce his presence wherever he went, a refinement made possible by the elimination of the huge amplifier that had been installed under the dash on previous models.

This particular evening, he was not happy about leaving home. His life had taken an exciting turn and he had things to do before it changed forever, yet he could not ignore Cassie's plea that he meet with her now. He wondered what all the mystery was about; she had said only that it was important and that she had to see him. He had urged her to tell him about it over the phone, hoping to perhaps avert some interminable discussion over nothing; but she refused, instead insisting that they meet where they often did, in the third booth from the south side entrance of Benjy's Butter Burgers on Douglas.

He thought about her call as he slowly, albeit somewhat noisily, backed out of the driveway, feeling the rush he always did at the car's smoothly gliding movement; it was kind of like cruising on an air cushion.

What could it be that she didn't want to tell him over the phone? He wondered if this were not just another of the dramatic fantasies she indulged in from time to time, in which she was a damsel in distress facing dire consequences without quick and dramatic action on the part of the hero in her plots, a part usually relegated to Rick in the six months she had been his steady girl. During the past two semesters, she had tried on numerous occasions to entice him into trying out for the productions staged by the school's drama department, usually comical, ham-handed farces in which the hero (him, if he got the part) would ride (usually) to the rescue of the beautiful, imperiled heroine (Cassie, of course) just before the ax fell or the pyre was lit.

But melodrama was Cassie's interest, and she was really quite good at it, having played nearly identical parts in three student-written-and-produced plays over the course of the school year. He himself would have none of it, believing, as Dirty Harry put it, "a man ought to know his limitations."

He had been working at Benjy's the night he and Cassie met, his thoughts at the time occupied with the new tailpipe he would buy with his week's wages. She had come in with a friend and sat at what they now considered "their" table. He noticed her right away; somehow she seemed different from the other girls who passed in and out of the burger joint. She was pretty, although most of them were pretty. But Cassie had a smile that lit up the room. When he brought their order and she looked up at him, he knew then he wanted to see her again—a lot. When she and her friend left, he ran after them to the parking lot and asked for her phone number. He remembered how her friend giggled when Cassie wrote it on the menu he didn't know he had in his hand. She was his girl from then on.

So what would he be saving her from now? The thought that it could be anything more profound than a choice of accessories for prom night never crossed his mind; in fact, it was the one thing that would be just like her. Now he thought about that event too, just two weeks away, as he turned right on Spring and headed east. Oncoming headlights created a near blinding glare through the slightly oily film that covered his windshield in spite of several attempts to clear it with the new washer fluid he had used the last time he filled the reservoir; he made a mental note to avoid that bargain brand in the future. But right now he was anxious to get this meeting over with, and also to surprise Cassie with his own news when he saw her.

That news began just last Saturday, when he and Buzz were hanging out at the mall. Buzz was probably his best friend, and the two had spent much of their free time together, at least when they weren't making it a foursome with Cassie and Buzz's girl Julie. Many times he had listened to his friend recount his troubles with parents who, in his somber and youthful assessment of their restrictions, didn't understand him.

"They just don't get it," he would say on numerous occasions, usually when they refused to underwrite some adventure he had in mind, like the class outing that had been organized to Fort Lauderdale last year. Buzz and half the junior class planned a week-long vacation at the popular resort area and planned to stay at a rented condo on the beach, sharing expenses. To Buzz, there were no problems; after all, if the other parents approved, why should his object? The stumbling block turned out to be Mike Stoner, a dropout who knew the condo's owners, and that they would be at home in Chicago during the week the kids planned to stay there. He had assured everyone he had permission, and even encouragement, to use the spot for the school break. Mike had been a hanger on with Buzz's crowd since he left school—some say was kicked out—after a brush with the law. Mike and a couple of his rowdier friends had broken into an empty vacation cottage on the peninsula sometime over that last winter. The end result was that they trashed the house during a party and during which the police were alerted by a neighbor who was also a year-round resident, and was well aware of the schedules of his sno bird neighbors. Mike and the others were apprehended and faced a number of charges, most of which were dropped when their collective parents agreed to make full restitution to the cottage's owner, leaving the miscreants with fines and probation. Once Mike's involvement in the planned vacation escapade became known, Buzz's parents refused to even consider allowing their son to participate; and when Buzz later assured them that Mike had dropped out of the arrangements and would no longer be part of the group, they remained unconvinced, and refused to budge on any further consideration of their son's anticipated Florida caper.

Buzz had been disappointed at their decision, particularly when he had been looking forward to some time on his own, making his own decisions, his first real encounter with adult responsibility. But though he had sulked awhile after their refusal, it didn't matter after all; the plan fell through when Mike was caught speeding and an open bottle of whiskey, plus a few marijuana joints, were discovered in the back seat of his car. Naturally, Mike denied they were his, but his story didn't work, and this time he was sentenced to a short term in a nearby youthful offender correctional institution.

None of this dampened Buzz's determination to prove he wasn't a kid anymore, a desire with which Rick heartily identified and concurred as they meandered along the store fronts. At the entrance to the Navy recruiting office, Buzz dropped back to examine their display, and Rick, who hadn't noticed his friend's detour, walked on for a distance before he became aware that he was talking to himself. Retracing his steps, he rejoined his friend and, taking in the exciting posters and patriotic fervor of the advertisements, knew without being told exactly what Buzz was thinking.

"C'mon, Buzz. Carson's is having another going-out-of-business sale and I want to look at their leather jackets. Everything is seventy-five percent off, and I've still got the gift card I got for my birthday. I might find something really neat."

But Buzz was mesmerized by the opportunity he saw reflected in the glittering depictions of derring-do that covered the walls of the display. *That could be me*, he thought, picturing himself in the cockpit of a jet fighter or on the deck of a destroyer. Suddenly, he saw a way out of a situation he felt was crowding his space.

"No, wait a minute. We've got plenty of time to make the sale. Let's hear what they have to say. It won't hurt to just listen. Come on. Come with me," Buzz pleaded, motioning toward the two recruiters who were seated behind desks in the office, which they could see through the open doorway.

"Please, Rick. I really want to look into this. It might be the answer to a lot of things for me; maybe you, too. Come on in; it won't hurt to just listen. It won't take long. Come on."

Just talk, that's all he planned to do and as far ahead as he thought at the time, and he persuaded Rick to listen in. Both were unprepared, however, for the persuasiveness of the local Naval recruiter; two hours later, they had become part of his monthly quota and would leave for basic training the week after graduation—at least Buzz would for sure, because he had just turned eighteen, while Rick was three months shy of his eighteenth birthday and still needed his parents' permission to enlist.

Rick's head began swimming as soon as they left the office and he realized what he'd done.

"Buzz, this is heavy, man. We shouldn't have done it. We should never have gone in there. Two years. *Two years*, man. And that could be just the start. It could be four years. That's a long time, man. It's just about an eternity, I guess."

"You said it. Ain't it great? Wow, I can't wait to get a load of my old man's face when I tell him. He'll about burst! And Mom'll be on the phone with her sisters the rest of the day. I'm free, man. *Free.* They wouldn't let me go to *Florida*, for cripes' sake. Wait until they find out where I'm going now! And I can't wait. I wish I could leave right now!" his friend answered cheerfully.

Rick forgot about the sale at Carson's and just wanted to get some fresh air. He wanted to go home. He was uneasy thinking about everything the recruiter had told them, especially what the man had said about basic training. He had never been away from home before, at least, not really; he was pretty sure the half hour drive across the county line to his Aunt Carol's home in Kenosha didn't count.

Once home, he went to his room and lay on the bed studying the ceiling, not sure what had really happened that afternoon. They were just going to listen; there weren't supposed to be any commitments.

Now he had agreed to a minimum of two years, maybe four. But what a time it would be. He could go to school, get advanced training when he decided on a field of interest; and the travel, all over the world; then the man went on about pay and benefits, and it all sounded better than anything he had even imagined on those few times he actually contemplated his own future. *It's not set in stone—not yet; I can still back out*, he thought. Nothing was for sure until his parents okayed the papers. *Maybe they'll refuse.* His head continued to spin with the window of possibilities that had just opened for him.

When he finally found the courage to approach his parents with the papers they would have to sign, his dad read them over without a word while his mom collapsed into a nearby chair. Rick listened nervously as they discussed this new development, his future pinned to their words and ultimate decision.

"Well, Ida, what do you think?" his dad asked when his mother recovered enough to maintain a conversation.

"I don't know, Jim. It's a big step. It's the first time he'll be on his own. It may be just over the state line from us, but it may as well be a world away. And he's so young, Jim. He's just so very young."

"I know. It'll be a change, that's for sure. But I think it may well turn out to be the best thing that could have happened. He'll be on his own, sure, but in the short term, he'll be able to call and we'll certainly see him during his training period. Afterward he may be sent elsewhere, but maybe that's a good thing, too. Let him see a little of the rest of the world. If he liked it enough to stay in, it would make a fine career. And you can't deny the opportunities and benefits outweigh what he could expect in most jobs around here, assuming he can find one in the first place with no real education or experience. No, Ida, I think that right now, this is a good thing. It might turn out to be the best thing that could happen."

And so, while they were certainly taken aback, in a way they were relieved, too. Rick had been lackadaisical about his future plans, unable—or unwilling—to make any kind of decision for his life after graduation; they now began to hope his upcoming tour of duty would be just the thing to help him settle down and think a bit, perhaps get a clearer idea of just where his life was headed. They both recognized that the opportunities the service offered exceeded any prospects he currently had to look forward to.

With the initial shock over, and the prospect of a positive outcome to their son's impulsiveness, they became as excited as he was and proud of him as well; and so, with a slight hesitation and some anxious reluctance, they signed his enlistment papers and began planning his going away party. The signed papers were returned to the recruiting office the following morning. Rick's father went along and spent a few minutes talking to the recruiter who had signed his son; he left with a copy of the papers and a sense of reassurance that they had indeed done the right thing.

Rick felt his life had become a muddled blur, and he had not thought to tell Cassie of its newest development, which would surely rival her wildest imaginings. Besides, he had tried to call her—twice—but her phone had been uncharacteristically silent; he had been unable to even leave a message. He would have to tell her when they met.

The throbbing cadence of *Hey, Soul Sister* boomed as Rick turned left onto Douglas. Cruising past the dizzy neon lights that lined the main drag and bounced off the highly polished hood, he wondered what he would do with the car while he was away. The thought of selling it never occurred to him. Sell the Chevy? To Rick's young mind, that was tantamount to sacrilege. He had been lucky enough to find the car when he passed his driving test at sixteen. Oh, there had been restrictions on his license, but it didn't matter. He could get a car; his dad had said so. They scoured the want ads for months, checking out one old wreck after another, until they found it—a 1957 Chevy 150 series two door sedan, Midnight Blue—at an estate sale. The owner intended to restore it, but died before he got very far. The executor of the estate, a lawyer, didn't want to bother with it and ordered it sold—period. So when Rick's dad made an offer of three hundred dollars, to their amazement it was accepted. It even ran, and Rick drove it home that very day, growling from a hole in the muffler and blue smoke spiraling out of the tailpipe. It was a sorry sight that first day in the driveway, but it was his. Most of his wages from his part-time job at the drive-in went for parts to rebuild the engine and reinforce the suspension; money gifts for his birthday and Christmas helped pay for body work. He and Buzz spent the majority of their free time working on the car, haunting junk yards and any private sales where car parts were advertised. Sometimes the girls came along on these jaunts, and the four of them would make a party of it, celebrating with pizzas at the end of a successful outing. But it was worth it, all of it. The car was a beauty and the pride of his life. But what would happen when he had to leave?

That dilemma was soon resolved. There was just enough space beside the garage in the rear yard—he could leave it there, maybe up on blocks or something. That would work. He would need a car when he came home on leave, as the recruiter had assured him he would, assuming in his innocence that would surely be weekends and holidays; after all, the training center was just over the state line, right on the Amtrak route, hardly the end of the world. He could get a ride to and from the local station and take the train right to the base; it only took an hour, two at the most. It wasn't far at all.

Another mile or so and the pounding rhythm of *Nothin' On You* heralded his arrival at Benjy's bright orange pulsing star. Picking a space at the rear of the near-empty lot, Rick parked and turned the key; the engine and radio fell simultaneously silent; he sauntered to the door and entered. Tonight Benjy's usually raucous crowd was eerily absent.

Rick stood inside the door for a moment and looked around. Cassie was sitting alone at their favorite table, forlornly staring down at its laminated top. She looked tired, more so than he was used to seeing her, or maybe it was the way she sat kind of slumped over her small Coke, her fingers running up and down the cup. His school jacket—he could see his varsity letter on the left sleeve—was draped around her shoulders. He had given her the jacket during a cool night at the lake front and then forgotten about it when he took her home, and somehow ever since. Surely she didn't need it now. As he got closer, he noticed that her honey-blonde hair, streaked with platinum-something, needed combing; the color on her lips was pretty much worn off, too.

Cassie hadn't seen him enter or approach the booth, but raised her eyes to meet his when he slid into the seat opposite her. She studied his face for a minute with a look that held him silent. And then she began to cry.

- The End -

-The Case Of The Pilfered Painting -

In the small, cluttered back room of the Grey Goose Bookstore on the corner of Market and Phinney in downtown Seattle, in a recently cleared space on a sturdy wooden table amid boxes of new arrivals awaiting his attention, Joshua's knife paused above a carton of books he was preparing to check in, the result of the latest auction at Digby & Sons.

The carton had been their Lot No. 42, on which he had bid sight unseen; it was this inability to examine parcels of odd-lot books which had resulted in a lack of interest among the other buyers on the day of the auction.

Now Joshua stood wondering if perhaps the eclectic selection of hard-covered volumes might possibly contain a rare first edition or two, or perhaps even something on his current customer want list. Usually this was not the case, and the assortment would most likely wind up on the shop's closeout table during the District's next sidewalk sale.

His musing regarding his latest acquisition was interrupted when Henrietta breezed through the door, punctual as ever, smartly dressed in a casual summer suit and carrying a box from Angelo's bakery on Yesler. Joshua immediately steeled himself for the barrage of tittle-tattle that he was sure would soon fill the small shop.

"You'll never guess who I ran into when I stopped at Angelo's this morning for their sponge cake...you know, the layered kind you like so much?...the one they make special on Tuesdays?" she called out through the open door.

She was right, Joshua thought absentmindedly—he would never guess—although he was happy to learn she had brought his favorite dessert, a four-tiered wonder filled with the bakery's signature crema pasticcera filling.

Henrietta proceeded to the small mahogany card table with the tile inlay top that served as their snack room; there she began to unwrap her purchase.

Oblivious to Joshua's lack of response to her opening salvo, she called out, "Goodness gracious, it was Lauren Harper, of all people. You know Lauren, the potter who turns out such wonderful pieces in the barn she converted into a workshop on that little farm out Newcastle way, the one she inherited from her grandfather? Well, anyway, she and I got to talking you see, and she told me that her attorney, that handsome Mr. Carmody, had arranged for an audit after her aunt's will was read; I imagine that sort of thing is standard procedure with an estate as expansive as her aunt's—her husband, Lauren's uncle, was in lumber, you know."

Silence reigned for just a moment; Joshua assumed she had stopped to catch her breath; but that was not the case. Henrietta had moved to the doorway, and her usual whiny, singsong voice took on an almost conspiratorial tone as she all but whispered, forcing Joshua to freeze where he stood, lest any movement drown out her now subdued words.

"Would you believe it, Joshua? That exquisite painting her aunt left her—the little one, about eight by eleven, by that famous Italian artist Canaletto—he's dead, of course—that little street scene—I mean, I've only seen it once, when Lauren lent it to a fund raiser for the museum; you remember, I helped with the refreshments that evening; but, my word, it was simply breathtaking, not to mention practically priceless? Well, it has simply vanished—*vanished*, I tell you," she said with special emphasis.

Henrietta continued in the strident tone her voice always assumed whenever she was excited, a high, tinny pitch which never failed to grate on Joshua's nerves.

"Lauren said they positively scoured every nook and cranny of her aunt's enormous Victorian—I joined Lauren there for lunch when we were both on some committee, I remember the place was a nightmare of halls and rooms galore—it's been standing vacant all this time while they catalog and prepare the contents for auction; auction, Joshua, because the woman was a hoarder and the house was filled to the ceilings with objet d'art she and her husband had collected during their very lengthy marriage—they loved to travel and went simply everywhere at one time or another, you know—and, well, they couldn't find it."

To Joshua's relief, Henrietta's voice resumed its normal whiny lower decibel singsong as she went on, "Simply everything was listed on one insurance policy or another, don't you know. The Canaletto even had its very own rider, but when they tried to check it off, there was another painting hanging in its place, one Lauren had never seen; she was very familiar with the work and recalled exactly where it should have been; but it wasn't there, Joshua—it wasn't there! Mr. Carmody notified the police, of course, and that friend of yours, that nice Detective Hollings—the one who devours Grisham?—is looking into the matter. What do you think of that?"

Taking advantage of Henrietta's pause to finally replenish her air supply, Joshua carefully slid the knife through the shipping tape, laid it aside, and slowly, his attention fully focused on the task at hand, opened the carton before replying.

"Any suspects?" he called out, knowing he did not have much time before she would be off again. He barely got the comment out before Henrietta once again plunged onward with her latest piece of delicious goings on.

"Apparently not right off," she told him, once again at full volume, "but I wouldn't want Jack Hollings on my trail, I can tell you. I wouldn't be able to sleep not one wink, that's for sure. He's certain to question just everyone. Doesn't it make you want to be a fly on the wall? Who do you think could possibly have taken it? And when, not to mention why. And surely someone must have, because Lauren said there was simply no other way to explain it not being in the house.

That's where it was kept, you know, valuable as it was, so her aunt could see it whenever she wanted, how it comforted her after her grandfather passed a few years ago, that was the only reason it was kept in the house at all, don't you know."

Before he could answer, and seemingly without the need for a breath, she said adamantly, "Exercise in futility, that's what I say. Imagine trying to palm off a thing like that. Why, it's worth an absolute fortune. In fact, I have it, from a very reliable source mind you, that the painting was insured for a half million dollars; nowhere it's true value, of course, but still, *a half million dollars*, Joshua. What do you think of that?"

Sorting through dog-eared volumes on architectural theory that disappointingly comprised the major portion of the shipment, Joshua murmured, "I'm sure Jack will sort it out." His attention started when he noticed an aged Agatha Christie mystery—a first edition, he was sure of it. Tenderly caressing the volume, his enthusiasm evaporated when he checked the inside print list and realized the book was indeed a first edition—unfortunately by an American publisher. "Worthless," he mumbled to himself, continuing to rummage through the rest of the volumes in the carton.

Henrietta had managed to make a fresh pot of coffee without missing a beat in her reiteration of her conversation with the young heiress. Settling in at the table for two behind the stacks in a corner of the shop proper, she poured a cup for each of them to accompany the cake wedges she had deposited on delicate porcelain dessert plates. Joshua, meanwhile, had made his way to a wall shelf across the room from the table where Henrietta awaited him; there he deposited his reading glasses before joining his assistant for their morning break.

"I'm sure you're right, Henrietta," he said thoughtfully, settling himself in his chair before savoring the cake's luscious cream filling—ambrosia for sure. "The disappearance of the painting will certainly be in the news, no doubt along with a very good description.

I doubt anyone who might consider its purchase could claim to not know it was stolen property."

"I should say not," Henrietta agreed, a bit indignantly, making a mental note of Joshua's glasses in order to remind him of their location when he invariably asked her later if she had seen them. "I do wonder, though, who might have taken it and just how long it's been missing. And where could it possibly be now do you think?"

"I couldn't possibly fathom a guess," Joshua replied, his mind again occupied with the remaining volumes he had yet to catalog.

"It had to be someone Lauren knows, I would imagine," Henrietta mused. "Wouldn't you say so, Joshua?"

Before he could venture an opinion at this opportunity, she went on, "It would have to be someone familiar with the house, of course. Someone in the family? Unthinkable. I mean, how could they? No, it had to be someone with a reason to visit the house, perhaps while her aunt was ill. I should think people were coming and going quite a bit about then. Now let's see...," Henrietta paused, her cup suspended in midair, as she mentally ran down the list of probable suspects and their likely culpability.

Suddenly, her face paled. She set her cup down carefully and looked across the table at Joshua. She noticed the darkened areas on the sleeves of his sweater from his inadvertent dusting of the shelves each time he rearranged the volumes. Then she said solemnly, "You know, Joshua, it just struck me. What if there's a connection between Mrs. Harper's death and the disappearance of that painting? Do you suppose that's possible?" she asked, her eyes wide.

"I don't think so, Henrietta," he assured her. "Don't forget, Mrs. Harper was up in age and not in the best of health. I believe the article in the Times explained that Mrs. Harper had been doctoring quite a bit in those last few months before Lauren found her when she returned from some errands that day. According to the story, the inquiry at the time determined that her heart had simply stopped sometime when she dozed off after Lauren left. Moreover, you said they have no idea as to when the painting was actually taken; it could have been anytime, and therefore by anyone. As I recall, Lauren had said it was kept at the house only as a remembrance of her grandparents' last trip to Italy; that's when they acquired it, as I understand. Although where something that valuable would be safe, I certainly wouldn't know."

"Yes, yes," Henrietta said impatiently, fingering the pince-nez that hung from her neck on a black braided cord, "but it's really just too intriguing. It has all the ingredients of a first-rate crime novel, if you ask me. Think of it, Joshua: a young heiress alone and grief stricken after the mysterious death of her aunt; a painting, a treasured legacy, missing; the police baffled."

Henrietta's eyes gleamed as her mind raced. Rapt with imagination, she was quiet for a moment. Then she looked around the shop at the neatly arranged shelves of paperbacks and hard covers, at the courtesy coffee island with its stacks of paper cups, packets of sugar and powdered creamer, and she said, "By the way, Joshua, the sleeves of that sweater need attention. Do let me rinse it out for you as soon as it's convenient. I could take it home with me tonight and have it back to you by the weekend."

The directional change in her line of thinking startled him, although he knew she was right—his sweater needed freshening; it had simply been handy and the last thing he reached for that morning before heading downstairs to open the shop. Perhaps he would avail himself of her offer; he had to admit she handled his sweaters beautifully; he could never get the blocking thing as precisely as she did, and it made all the difference between a serviceable sweater and a ruined one.

"I suppose you're right, Henrietta," he agreed amiably, as he usually did, if only to avoid disturbing the tranquility he so treasured in the little shop. "But while the matter of the sweater is within our province to correct, I fear we must leave the larger issue in Jack's hands."

"How would you have done it?" she suddenly asked.

"Oh, cold water to be sure, with some of that special soap for fine woolens," he replied, unaware he had diverged from her latest line of thought.

"No, no," she exclaimed, "not the sweater, you dunderhead—the painting! How would you have engineered its disappearance? If you had, that is."

Joshua looked at her over the rim of his cup, mentally reconfiguring his thoughts before venturing to speak again. "Oh, that," he muttered, searching for an answer that would satisfy Henrietta's heightened excitement at this latest occurrence involving their occasional, but very good, customer. "I'm sure I wouldn't know. I'd have to put my mind to it, that's for sure."

"Oh, Joshua," she blurted in exasperation. "It's just as well you're not the guilty party. You most likely would have provided a crumb trail to the front door." She took a deep breath and retired within her private musings regarding the crime.

The following week found Henrietta in an unusually pensive mood. Joshua understood that although she was her usual efficient self, handling the various requests for reprints and best sellers and doggedly chasing down obscure tomes with aplomb, only a part of her intellect needed to be engaged in these endeavors. He could tell she was still intent on the ins and outs of the latest intrusion into their staid and orderly world—a crime had occurred that touched one of the shop's customers and, by extension of a wider arc, themselves. Hour after hour, Henrietta mechanically went through the motions of her duties, yet all the while her mind focused on the one point of information that would not allow it to rest: Who did it?

The following Wednesday was especially busy for a weekday, with no lull in customer traffic until an hour before closing, when Jack Hollings entered in response to Joshua's notice regarding not his usual Grisham, but a new Clancy that Joshua heartily recommended. The two exchanged pleasantries in the stacks at the back of the shop, after which Jack approached the cash register where Henrietta waited to check out his purchase. Joshua knew what was coming, and pointedly set about tidying the displays after the day's activity.

"Good afternoon, Sergeant Hollings," Henrietta began brightly. Joshua cringed. *Poor Jack.*

Her particularly friendly tone instinctively raised the detective's guard. "Hello, Henrietta. How are you?" he said cautiously, wondering what she was up to.

"I'm just fine, thank you, Jack," she replied. *Here it comes*, Joshua thought, and he was indeed correct. "But I was just wondering about Lauren Harper's painting. When I saw her last week, she mentioned how it simply could not be found during an inventory, the one taken for the audit after her aunt's death. Have you made any progress on the case?"

Now Hollings braced himself for the onslaught he knew was coming, for his activities, both progressive and otherwise, had been the target of Henrietta's scrutiny in the past when any sort of mischief occurred within his jurisdiction.

"Well, we're certainly making inquiries," he answered warily. "I'm sure we'll unravel the mystery in good time."

"Are you now," she said suspiciously. "And just what have you determined is the scope of the mystery you intend to solve in such good time?"

Hollings was trapped. Apprehensive of the point of her question, he asked, "What do you mean?"

"Well, just what are you dealing with? Mrs. Harper dying, the painting missing, and no one knows anything about it? Am I the only one who wonders if the two events might not be connected? Has it occurred to no one else that the poor woman may have been dispatched in the course of a robbery?"

"Mrs. Harper?" Oh Lord, she was going to light on that one.

"No, Henrietta, no connection at all. Really. The woman died of a heart attack, no mystery there; hardly unexpected, given her age. She was, after all, eighty-six years old."

"Perhaps," Henrietta allowed grudgingly. "But can you positively rule out a connection between the two events? Do you honestly believe that, absent a bullet or knife wound, murder is impossible? With the incentive of a painting valuable enough to be insured for a half million dollars?"

The reference surprised him. *How on earth did the blasted woman find out about the insurance?* He could not imagine the Harper girl discussing such a private financial matter.

"You're right, of course, Henrietta," he sighed. What else could he say? The truth was that initially no connection had been made between the two events, and with the body being cremated within days of the unhappy occurrence, there was no going back now.

"However, I assure you," he continued, "we are looking into all aspects of the situation. I'm confident the painting will turn up before too long, and when it does, it's just possible we may uncover more information regarding Mrs. Harper's death, in the unlikely event it was truly any more than natural causes."

The look Hollings got with his change told him Henrietta was not satisfied with his assurances. Well, he would just have to live with that. He took the bag with the book he had purchased and turned to leave. He had just taken hold of the door handle when he heard Henrietta behind him ask coyly, "And the helpful "lodger" who appeared seemingly out of nowhere to make himself practically indispensable to a lonely, but very wealthy, old woman in poor health? Surely you've spoken with him. What does he have to say?"

Hollings froze. He slowly released the handle and turned back to the register, where Henrietta was standing with her hand on her hip, a smirk surfacing on her face, as if she had thrown light on a blind spot the detective had not considered. Was this simply another of her maddening dead-end throw outs that had caused him no end of consternation in the past?

Hearing her unmistakable inflection on the word "lodger," Hollings asked, "Lodger? What lodger? You mean the kid staying there in return for a few odd jobs around the place? He's a pre-med student at the extension; when he's not in class he's studying his head off. Just what and how do you know about him, Henrietta?"

"Oh, really, Sergeant Hollings," she said condescendingly, the smirk indicating she realized she had scored a coup. Then, as if she were explaining the theory of relativity to a first grader, she said, "I've given the matter a good deal of thought, you know, and I've determined it was certainly someone close to Lauren, someone in her immediate circle of acquaintances, someone familiar with her aunt's house and her movements, and who knew not only the painting's existence, but its value and that it was kept in the library next to her grandfather's portrait."

Damn. Could there be something to what she was implying, or was she simply baiting him again? If not, is there anything the blasted woman doesn't know?

"That description could fit a lot of people, Henrietta. But go on," he told her with apparent resignation, in spite of a piqued interest at her outburst. Hollings did not take Henrietta to be a stupid woman—annoying perhaps...occasionally *very* annoying—and it would do no harm to hear her out, particularly since his own investigation had temporarily stalled due to a lack of any substantive clues at the Harper home.

"Well, consider," Henrietta began, giving voice to her recent musings, "to my mind there is just one person with access to the house who should be examined with particular care; in this case, a young man in financial difficulties with no immediate relief in sight, who had occasion to cultivate a lonely old woman, a woman who, in the course of frequent and seemingly caring get-togethers, had occasion to discuss her treasures, in particular an especially meaningful gift from her beloved grandfather: one small, valuable, easily transportable Canaletto."

Sergeant Hollings mentally ran down the members of the Harper family; no one fit the latest profile Henrietta had just described. Then he considered those outside the family, but close to it, with access to the house, and opportunities for the kind of ingratiation she also described. Well, there was someone, a long shot who, along with everyone else, had been interrogated and cleared. Still, ...

"Not...Jeremy?" he ventured cautiously.

"Bingo!" she confirmed.

Hollings slowly turned back to the door, exerted pressure on the handle, and resolutely walked through it. His mind was muddled by Henrietta's comments. *Lodger?* From her smirking inference, he knew the term had a special connotation, one he had to admit he blindly had not considered. But how the devil could she know? And why should she even think that Jeremy Hensholdt, a student enrolled in pre-med classes at the local university extension, might have had a nefarious intent when, as Lauren had explained, he had simply shown up at her aunt's home one day inquiring if there might be lodgings available in exchange for his services as a combination handyman/groundskeeper?

The kid definitely had not been overlooked during his investigation, Hollings assured himself, but had been questioned extensively along with everyone else; as Hollings recalled, Lauren stated that she had found her aunt dead on her return from her errands that day. She had visited her aunt several times a week, always unannounced, depending on her schedule, and called if she could not stop by. When could Jeremy have conducted his clandestine meetings to ingratiate himself with the old woman and Lauren been unaware of it? It was hard to imagine the scenario Henrietta recounted was at all likely.

Hollings began to suspect it was all a woman's intuition thing, and therefore to him completely incomprehensible. *And yet...?*

Hollings got into his car and started the engine, then paused. Could Henrietta be right? In interviewing the family and the few people with reason to visit the rambling old house on a regular basis, he had to admit what Henrietta said was distinctly within the realm of possibility...*the helpful lodger who appeared seemingly out of nowhere to make himself practically indispensable to a lonely, but very wealthy, old woman in poor health.* Her conclusion certainly wasn't inevitable; nevertheless, it was one he had failed to consider. Perhaps he needed to look again.

Joshua had heard the exchange between Jack and Henrietta, and wondered if he had just lost a customer. Would the detective return, or would he take his trade to another shop where he could escape being assailed by a relentless amateur?

"Don't you think that was a bit over the top?" he asked.

"Joshua," she began in a tone that dismissed any question of her conclusion, "think about it. College is expensive, for anyone. Professional courses are particularly expensive, and I would bet as surely as I would wager that the world will continue turning tomorrow that that young man already has, or surely will, accumulate a formidable amount of debt before he even graduates. That being the case, it is certainly conceivable that he would be susceptible to any situation that might substantially reduce his debt load. It would take a remarkable individual indeed to resist such a temptation, especially if he were convinced that he stood a good chance of getting away with it!" For emphasis, Henrietta slapped the register drawer shut, closing the discussion.

Henrietta saw no reason to enlighten either Joshua or Hollings as to the source of her apparent intuition. The truth was that the ladies normally present during her weekly appointments at Sally's Smart Set Salon followed the activities of Lauren Harper as faithfully as they perused the tales of celebrity goings on in the various tabloid publications to which the salon subscribed.

Among their group, all with standing appointments between one and three on Saturday, secrets were laid bare as surely as ice melted on a hot stove.

One regular, in the twelve-thirty slot and residing in an apartment building in Clyde Hill, recognized Jeremy's name from the Times article when the disappearance of the painting was first discovered and reported. Her nephew, a junior reporter on the paper, mentioned the insurance coverage on the painting; he said it was left out of the published report on the robbery as a privacy issue for Miss Harper. He requested the twelve-thirty keep that information to herself, which of course she did. She knew Jeremy only as a fellow tenant in her apartment complex, but remembers him as being constantly on the lookout for any scheme that would result in some kind of payout; big or small was no matter, all were regarded as contributions to his financial bucket.

Another, the one-fifteen, the wife of an attorney, recalled that Jeremy's name appeared in a case where one of the fraternities reported a shortage of funds. The matter was made a police affair when they attributed the loss to a theft which occurred while Jeremy was treasurer; however, nothing could be proven and the case was eventually dismissed without any charges ever being filed.

After the two o'clock, the manager of a lingerie shop who frequented Sally's for her monthly tints, mentioned rather expensive items selected by one Jeremy Hensholdt being sent to a Miss Glenda Bradley at the Clyde Hill address, and further mentioning that she only remembered the transaction because she wondered how a seemingly impecunious college student could afford the items he selected, and why someone of apparently limited means shopped in her admittedly exclusive establishment at all. Well, it wasn't difficult to fill in the blanks and reach the very conclusion Henrietta had just espoused.

The conversation with Henrietta haunted Sergeant Hollings in the following days as he renewed his interviews with the Harper clan, all of whom once again disavowed any knowledge of the theft or the present whereabouts of the painting, and with the student, who had left the Harper home soon after the old woman's death and was once again residing at his old Clyde Hill apartment complex. Hollings had dutifully tracked him down, only to find he had a convincing alibi, having arranged to have his presence witnessed in the campus library the afternoon Lauren was away on her errands. *And yet...?*

Hollings wondered about Henrietta's apparent conviction that there was a player outside the sphere of the family and the occasional visitor to the house. Could she be right? He grudgingly suspected she was. It then occurred to him that perhaps he was not asking the right questions, and that a little backtracking might be in order. There were ways to obtain information other than direct confrontation.

A week went by, then another, with no information in the Times regarding the recovery of Lauren Harper's painting, and no further word from Jack. Henrietta trolled her usual haunts for any salient bits of gossip regarding new developments in the investigation and came up empty. It was as if the entire episode had simply never happened.

On the Monday morning of the third week after Henrietta's conversation with Jack, a small floral arrangement arrived at the shop. Joshua signed for the flowers and looked at the card for a long time. *Don't tell me...no, it couldn't be,* he thought. But what other explanation was there? None. *And yet...how?*

Henrietta immediately spied the arrangement when she arrived with Angelo's daily special, cannoli. Upon reading the accompanying card, her face took on a look of such self-satisfaction that Joshua was sure she would now be more impossible than ever, and steeled himself once more for the onslaught of her opinionated ranting. It never came. Instead, a calm settled over her, as if a great internal strife had suddenly been amiably resolved. He didn't get it, not until Hollings' visit later that afternoon.

Jack appeared at his usual time—an hour before closing—when the activity of the day had mainly dissipated and only a few browsing stragglers remained in the store. Joshua and Henrietta were arranging the display of a new shipment of best sellers when he walked in. Spying the flowers he had sent, which Henrietta had placed on the counter beside the register as a conversation incentive with every customer she checked out, he smiled and approached their display.

"Good afternoon, Jack," Joshua said cordially. Henrietta only nodded acknowledgment, yet she appeared about to burst with a look of "I told you so!"

"Good afternoon," Jack started, addressing them both. "I suppose by now you've guessed what happened. We've recovered the Harper painting, thanks in no small part to you, Henrietta."

With uncharacteristic modesty, Henrietta simply said, "I'm pleased to have been of help, Sergeant. How did you find it?"

A sheepish Jack Hollings related the new direction his investigation had taken after Henrietta's comments. He began reviewing purchases billed to the private checking account of Jeremy Hensholdt, supposedly average college student.

A number of suspicious items, among them designer lingerie and imported liquor, had been sent to the apartment of one Glenda Bradley in Clyde Hill, a Seattle suburb on the other side of Lake Washington. It was this wish to please and impress the Bradley girl with offerings beyond the meager financial limits of his scholarship that contributed to Jeremy's chronic dearth of funds.

A cursory investigation revealed that Miss Bradley waited tables at a small pub near the college that was a popular hangout for its students; it was there she had first met Jeremy. Miss Bradley initially denied any knowledge of Jeremy's activities at the Harper household before he left that employer to share her apartment. She claimed the gifts were simply acknowledgments of various milestones in their relationship. However, once presented with the matter of the disappearance of a valuable work of art and its possible connection to the death of Lauren's aunt, the entire story slowly emerged.

According to Miss Bradley, Jeremy was indeed drowning in debt, and had frequently lamented the amount of time it would take him to resolve the matter and begin to accumulate funds on his own behalf. Jeremy longed for the kind of comfortable lifestyle the Harpers enjoyed, and to which he had become accustomed while in their employ.

Jeremy had been given a key to the Harper house, so as to tend to various maintenance issues as his schedule permitted, and also to look in on Mrs. Harper during Lauren's absences. In the course of his frequent visits to the Harper home, many of which in Mrs. Harper's increasingly fading memory she invariably failed to mention when her niece called, Jeremy was able to peruse the old woman's treasures: they were a plentiful and assorted lot. He knew all were valuable originals of one sort or another; his problem was to select one that was unlikely to be missed in the short term. Should the item's disappearance be discovered sometime after his departure, he was sure there would be no way it could be traced to him, not if he were careful to cover his tracks in disposing of it.

But he had to make sure the item was valuable enough to justify the risk he would be taking, and to that end he feigned interest in everything of potential in the Harper home, and listened eagerly to Mrs. Harper's sketchy descriptions of the various pieces, what little she recalled of how and where they were acquired, and her at best unreliable guess at the approximate value of each.

His interest eventually focused on the Canaletto when a little research verified its suspected value, and he set about locating a potential buyer who would not be too particular regarding the painting's previous owner. This was not particularly difficult for someone as clever and determined as Jeremy Hensholdt, and he soon had a buyer in place with cash in hand.

Certain that no one would miss one small item amid the jumble of collectibles that filled the old house, Jeremy put his plan into operation. He watched for an appropriate opportunity to replace the painting in question with a similarly sized and fashioned one of no importance that he had managed to acquire during a haunt of local antique dealers; then he simply bided his time, which came when Lauren left one afternoon for a meeting at one of the studios that carried her work.

With the rambling structure temporarily devoid of anyone but its owner, Jeremy sought to insure he would not be seen. Having slipped out of the library unobserved to return to the house, he went to Mrs. Harper's room, where he believed she was probably resting, as he could not locate her anywhere else and he had never known her to leave the premises; he intended to peek in with the pretext that he was simply checking to make sure she was all right.

He found Mrs. Harper sitting in a rocker near a sunny window, seemingly asleep. But watching the old woman, Jeremy noticed that she did not appear to be breathing. He approached gingerly, expecting her to wake any second. She did not. He was not mistaken. She was, indeed, not breathing.

It was the opportunity Jeremy had been waiting for. He quickly switched the paintings and left the house to hurry back to the library, temporarily storing the work in the trunk of his car while he slipped back into the building, seemingly never having left.

Lauren returned that afternoon to find her aunt dead. Jeremy's explanation for his own absence was that he had been at the library, busily studying for an upcoming exam; he said he even blamed himself for Mrs. Harper's death, saying that if he had just taken a break to look in on her, perhaps he could have been in time to summon help.

According to Miss Bradley, the painting was later transferred to the buyer Jeremy had previously selected, whose name Miss Bradley claimed never to have known, as she also claimed not to know the disposition of the cash Jeremy received. According to her, he had simply told her that he couldn't risk depositing such a sizable amount, at least not so soon, but that it was in a safe place for the time being and they would enjoy it in due time.

Based on Miss Bradley's statement, a search warrant was obtained; on a hunch, Hollings specified Jeremy's locker on campus. Jeremy was called out of the lecture hall when the police arrived, and watched as they opened his locker, unzipped the gym bag he had hurriedly stowed inside, and discovered bundles of cash in a variety of high denominations. Hollings had stretched his hunch to include an arrest warrant, and Jeremy was taken into custody immediately. Over coffee at headquarters, Jeremy reluctantly confessed everything.

"You know, funny thing about the kid," Hollings remarked. "It wasn't the discovery of his scheme that bothered him; he admitted he had almost been expecting it; but he was totally crushed by the Bradley girl's betrayal. And here's the kicker," Hollings said with an amused look on his face, "the money that was going to treat the two of them to a whole new life? It was counterfeit!"

"Counterfeit?" Joshua and Henrietta blurted in tandem.

"Absolutely," Hollings continued.

"You see, Jeremy was a bright boy," he went on to explain, "but compared to the people he was dealing with in trying to palm off the painting, he was a rank amateur, a real piker, in no way a match for people who make a profitable enterprise out of trading in stolen artifacts of all types, including pilfered Canalettos, and the only surprise is that Jeremy managed to stumble upon someone that sophisticated in the first place.

"Fortunately, when Jeremy saw the error of his ways, he identified his contact, who was in the process of transferring the painting to a contact of his own; I guess he never figured us to move as quickly as we did. We caught up with him heading for the state line, and picked him up along with the painting. We'll return it to Miss Harper as soon as the paperwork is complete. Jeremy's contact will be with us a bit longer—quite a bit longer, actually. And it's just too bad Jeremy wasn't able to do a bit of research on his "collector," or he would have found him on the FBI Ten Most Wanted list with a considerable reward for information leading to his arrest and conviction, a reward that would have gone a long way in solving Jeremy's financial situation. Funny how some things work out."

At the conclusion of his story, the three were silent, each ruminating over the developments Hollings had described. Finally, Henrietta broke their collective reverie. "Well, Sergeant, now that things are back to normal, I suppose you'll have some time on your hands." Selecting the latest Grisham novel from their carefully arranged display, she handed it to him and said simply, "Will that be cash or charge?"

- The End –

- A Change Of Plan -

Merk Tandy and Hawley Crawford sat in the dimly lit corner of a dingy saloon in a no-name town near the Colorado border. As Hawley eyed the poker game at the next table, Merk read and reread the piece of paper in his hands. <u>Ten thousand dollars.</u> He tried to imagine that amount of money. <u>Ten thousand dollars.</u> It was more money than he had ever seen, more than he had ever even dreamed of.

"We could do it, Hawley," he said. "We could get us this here money. You and me, we'd split it fifty-fifty. This here poster says he might be travelin' with this Sammey fella, that's two thousand more for him. Hawley, this here's <u>twelve thousand dollars.</u> Let's see now...that'd be six thousand dollars for each of us if we took 'em both. I could do a lot with six thousand dollars, Hawley, and so could you. I say we go lookin' for these two."

Hawley Crawford turned his attention to his companion. Merk Tandy was about his own height, which wasn't too tall. His stringy black hair needed cutting, something he usually tended to himself. Merk had a thin face with the biggest nose Hawley'd ever seen. Had it broke enough times, too, usually after getting them involved in schemes like the one he was thinking about now. Merk had been pulling the folded poster from his shirt, reading it over and over, ever since he tore it off a wall in the last town they'd come through. Hawley didn't rightly recall the name, except it had something to do with direction. Seemed a nice enough little town though. They had been low on grub and stopped for supplies when Merk spied the poster and ripped it off the wall; he had talked of nothing else since.

"Where you figure to look, Merk? It says them fellas could be all through this territory. It ain't like we had nothing to do but go lookin' for 'em. We have to get us some money, and I mean real soon. My last dollar went for those fixins' we bought back there. I ain't got no more. We need money now, Merk; we need it real bad."

"I know, Hawley, I know. But that's just it. I'm right tired of needin' money and havin' no way to git none. And this here's more money than we'll likely ever see in our whole lives, Hawley, and you know that's the truth."

Hawley was a thin man, not young anymore, and not well either. He'd made his way just drifting ever since he could remember. He and Merk met on a ranch where they both had hired on to wait out the winter. The money they made there was more than either of them had had in a long while. Of course, that was most likely because they had no place to spend it. As soon as spring came, they both quit. They took the checks they had saved up over those long wintry months and cashed them in; once they hit town, they quickly made up for any real or perceived deprivations they had endured.

Now Hawley often thought about their time on that ranch, and as often as he thought about it, he wished he had stayed there. He and Merk had it good, better than in a long time. He liked his boss, for the first time in just about ever, the chores were fair, and the grub was mighty good and plentiful, even Merk had agreed on that.

But Merk had heard stories of silver strikes across the border in Colorado, stories that fired him up until he couldn't stop thinking about trying his own hand. Merk knew even less about mining than Hawley, which was not much at all, but the thought of all that silver just called to him so strong, he could think of nothing else. So he and Merk teamed up to see if they couldn't get a stake of their own.

The thing was, though, they never figured on looking for silver being so much work. They had pooled their money, at least what they had left by the time they reached the border, and bought a claim. The fella that owned it told them he had hauled out enough ore to live in style, and figured on taking it easy from then on, so he was selling out to give someone else a chance to make their fortune too. The fella hadn't looked all that prosperous to Hawley, who said as much at the time.

But Merk had strike fever; he figured the fella had just been too busy making his money to have spent any of it.

So he and Merk broke rock and hauled dirt for three months and never took out enough ore to buy themselves a beer. Then Hawley's lungs just plain gave out. He got to coughing so bad he couldn't do much else. He gave what money he had to a doctor in a small town near their claim. The doc told him to stay out of the mine or the dust would kill him. He and Merk just drifted after that, working around wherever they could, earning just enough to get them to the next spread. Now they didn't even have that much.

The spirited bidding at the next table caught Merk's attention. Looking over at the six men involved in the game, he listened as they raised one another and added their money to the pile in the middle of the table. He looked at Hawley and saw that the action had caught his attention too. Several of the players had dropped out of the latest round and a vaquero was the last to bid. After all the cards had been placed face up on the table, the vaquero and another man each had full houses, hands higher than the others. But the vaquero was ace high, and as the others shrugged in disgust, he put his hands around the mound of coins in the middle of the table and pulled it in.

Merk and Hawley exchanged glances; each knew what the other was thinking: They sure could use that money. They were also of one mind about how to get it.

They finished their drinks and left the saloon, but did not go far. It was late. The night was starless and the only light was the faint glow from the saloon's grimy window. There were only two horses beside their own at the hitching post out front, so most of the players inside had to live somewhere nearby. Merk and Hawley stationed themselves on either side of the small adobe building and waited, hoping the vaquero did not play long enough to lose what he had won.

It seemed a long time before the saloon began to empty. In ones and twos the men who had sat around the table drifted out. The vaquero finally came out alone and turned to his left; he walked past the corner of the building where Merk had been waiting in the dark. He never heard the footsteps that came up behind him; he just felt a blow that brought him to his knees, and a second one that rendered him unconscious.

Hawley had come around the back of the building when he saw which way the vaquero was headed. Now they went through his pockets. Merk found the money the man had won, but they didn't stop there. They took the matched pistols he wore along with his fancy belt and spurs. Hawley wanted his boots, too, but Merk said they'd better git. The two of them casually returned to their horses, mounted up and cantered out of town.

When they made camp that night, they counted the money. Thirty dollars. It would be enough to start them on their way to the much larger windfall they now planned to collect.

* * *

"I tell you, Merk, I ain't goin' no more on this here trail. It ain't hardly wide enough for a man to pass walkin'. I thought we was trailin' rustlers—this look like cattle country to you? We got to go back."

Hawley had gone along with what had seemed like a good plan at the time. The owner of the only saloon in the last saddle-sore town they'd come through said he recognized the faces on the posters Merk had shown him; said they passed through maybe a month before. As far as he knew they headed north, at least he thought so, but he wasn't rightly sure. Anyway, it got Merk's blood up just finding someone who'd seen the wanted men. He figured he and Hawley were sure to be right behind them, even if the trail was a month old. But somehow they veered off toward mountains Hawley'd never seen the likes of, until some deep inexorable instinct told Hawley that if they were looking for rustlers, they would also be looking for cattle, and there just weren't no way cattle would be climbing the hills they were in now.

Merk grudgingly admitted that for once Hawley made sense, and reluctantly the two turned around, sure this time that their quarry had also skirted the mountain range, probably heading for the grasslands of Wyoming. There would be cattle there, and men who stole them, and that's surely where he and Hawley would find their fortune.

* * *

"Ya know, Merk, I been thinkin."

Merk Tandy turned his attention to his companion. They had camped that night on a grassy plain that seemed to go on forever. The trail that had once seemed so promising had petered out and grown cold. No one had seen the faces on the posters in the last two towns they'd passed. They didn't really know quite where they were. They had been drifting alongside what appeared to have been a good-sized stream, if it hadn't been the middle of a lengthy summer drought. Judging from the watermarks along the banks, the lack of rain had reduced a fair-sized run of water to little more than a shallow creek.

Maybe they should have stopped at that last hangdog town and seen about some work. Had to be somebody thereabouts needing a couple of hands; Lord knows they could use some money. But then it seemed to Merk that they could always use some money. He and Hawley had been together quite a spell now. They had hooked up back in Kansas two, maybe three years ago. At the time, they drifted together and stayed together because of their mutual interest in an easy dollar. At one time or another they'd tried both sides of the law, never striking a payload that afforded more than a stake to the next opportunity. And then it would start all over again.

They had worked towns some, ranched some, even tried their hands behind a badge once, in a little out-of-the-way town unaware of their wilder exploits; now, after all that time, neither one had a dollar saved nor a living soul waiting for them anywhere. Merk had an uneasy feeling it wasn't supposed to be that way. And now, Hawley had been thinking.

Tonight he thought Hawley looked more tired, or somehow maybe older, than usual. Suddenly Merk felt tired, and somehow maybe older, himself.

"What about, Hawley?" he asked, more to make conversation than anything else.

"Well, while you was askin' around about them posters in that town we just come from, I saw a map on the wall. It showed where we was just then. We're in Wyoming, Merk. According to that map on the wall back there, we're in Wyoming. That town back there was on the map; it showed it was just a spell south of the Platte River. Did you know that, Merk?"

"No, I didn't, Hawley. I surely didn't. What're you gettin' at?"

"That there river looked mighty big. I figure there's just got to be towns all up and down a river like that, maybe a railroad, too."

"Most likely." Merk watched Hawley's long thin face with its closely spaced brows knitted together as if forming a land bridge over his eyes. Hawley wasn't one to be thinking much, and Merk wondered what was occupying his mind now.

"Merk, that there town back there showed it to be just a little ways south of that Platte River. I figure we done rightly covered just about that amount of ground right now. I figure this here stream we been driftin' along is that there Platte River that showed on that map I seen."

"Well now, that's right smart figurin', Hawley. But what's it mean?"

"Dang it all, Merk, the way I look at it, ain't neither of us gettin' nowhere," his friend said with uncharacteristic vehemence. "Hell, truth is, we don't even know where we'll sleep next, or when we'll eat again. Now, you and me tried a lot of things to get along. Jus' seems to me don't nothin' ever work, least not for long. So what I been thinkin' is this: I'm gonna find me a railroad, and when I do, I'm gonna hop on and ride it clear to one of them there forts where the soldiers is, and I'm gonna join up."

Merk sifted through his partner's explanation, not immediately understanding just what Hawley was telling him.

"Join up? You mean the Army, Hawley? You sayin' you figure on signin' up an' joinin' the Army?"

"Yessir. That's what I mean, Merk. My mind's made up, too."

A momentary silence settled between them before Merk said, "I don't know, Hawley. Soldierin' ain't easy. In fact, it's right hard—ridin' all the time, in all kinds of weather. It gets hot out here, ya know, and mighty cold in the winter. An' what about them orders you gotta take all the time? An' it ain't like you can jus' walk out when the mood hits, either; I hear they shoot folks for that, Hawley, jus' for walkin' away. Don't seem that would suit me no how."

"Well, that's for you to say, Merk. But there's one thing I know for sure—them soldier boys don't go hungry, an' they get clothes better than we got, and horses better too, an' they don't always have to be wonderin' where they're gonna sleep at night. They jus' do what they're told, that's all; jus' do what they're told, and they get along jus' fine. Seems to me a right good life when you think about it, sure better than what we got now. I figure maybe I could learn to take the guff; others do and get along."

Merk was quiet, contemplating their campfire as he poked at it with a branch he'd found on the bank. He'd never put much store in Hawley's thinking before, but for the first time since they'd known one another, he had to admit that maybe this time his friend was right.

* * *

Among the passengers for the trip to Fort Mead were two scruffy-looking men who had boarded the train up the line a spell. The two had sold everything they had to pay for their tickets, with a little pocket money left over. Their horses and gear had brought a fair amount, but the real source of their temporary good fortune lay with a set of matched pistols and accessories they had presented for trade. The guns' silver inlays and intricately engraved stocks had obviously once been presentation caliber. The belt they adorned had a solid silver buckle with fancy Spanish scrollwork, the design being repeated on a matching pair of spurs. Real works of art the man at the dry goods emporium had called them, although he voiced despair at any prospect of selling them to local townspeople. He said he would, however, take the pieces in the hope of interesting one of the tradesmen who occasionally passed through town. The truth was that the items represented the finest workmanship he could remember seeing anywhere, and he was confident he would make a handsome profit on the decorative accoutrements. The buckle was a showy enough piece to bring a good price, but the spurs were unlike anything he had ever seen. He had read about a similar design, found particularly among vaqueros in California. They were the usual two-piece construction of shank and heel band, but this pair carried silver inlays on both sides. The engraved designs were intricate, the metal blued, and the edges of the heel bands were beveled. No, these were special, unlike the commoner designs put out by the local prison as part of its craft program.

The prison designs he was accustomed to seeing were heavier, both in material and engraving. Many of the inmates had worked on ranches at one time or another, so they were familiar with spurs, both their function and construction. Many of the spurs he came across were offered by cowpokes down on their luck. Often they were made of scrap iron from discarded ranch equipment. Not works of art, but functional. He had more of these than he cared for, but often would buy them for the price of a meal or a few drinks and sell them to another drifter in need of something just to get by. He could only guess at how the two had come into possession of such gear, but that wasn't his concern. He offered a fraction of what he knew to be the objects' true value, confident that desperate men had no choice but to be content with anything they could get.

The two now watched from their seats as passengers left the train and temporarily assembled on the platform; some of them were obviously expecting to be met and were looking around for familiar faces; others, apparently new to the town, paused momentarily to review their surroundings and gain their bearings. While new passengers boarded, freight and supplies were loaded onto empty cars for destinations east. There was a corral filled with cattle beyond the station headquarters, but little activity in the streets from what they could see.

Their attention turned to a group of men standing on the platform, waiting to board one of the forward cars. When they began to move toward the train, some of them shuffled forward. They were rumpled and unshaven, unlike their beardless images on the posters in the sheriff's office

One man, apparently in charge of the group from the glint of metal on his shirt pocket and whose movements were not hampered by restraints, turned to say something to his companion. The shifting of his body revealed a shotgun cradled in his left arm. Whatever was said, the other man nodded agreement.

Their interest piqued, the passengers watching through the window saw for the first time the shackles encircling the ankles of the shuffling prisoners, who remained a focus of attention until they were aboard and out of sight. Then one of the men broke the silence and gave words to what they both were thinking.

"You know, Hawley, them there prisoners could be us. Soldierin' don't look so bad no more."

"No, Merk, it sure don't," his companion agreed. "I just hope the food's good."

- The End -

- Covenant Of Blood -

"You're sure? There's no doubt?" Johan asked his father in a whispered tone.

"No doubt. It's starting," his father replied in a similarly hushed voice. "We must prepare him."

Johan, in his cassock and starched collar, shook his head and crossed himself. "God help him," was all he said.

"God help us all," his father added.

His father then looked at Jordan with pity and overwhelming sorrow, and began to explain the reason behind the changes that had come about in his formerly ordered life, changes which could not be denied, nor wished away, nor exorcised by any rite known to the church.

Vanpir!

At the very mention of the word in the old language, Jordan knew. He had become one of the undead. The unholy. He began to cry. *No! It can't be true*, he thought.

It began in the southern part of Silesia in the year 1739. His name wasn't Jordan then. In that long ago time he was Friedrich Hoffmann, the son of Otto Hoffmann, a tailor, and his wife, Greta. His family consisted of his parents and their nine children—seven boys and two girls. The girls and four of the boys died before their third year, leaving just Friedrich and his brothers, Johan and Anton. *Seven brothers, seven sons—of a father who was himself the last of seven brothers.*

"But why, father?" he had asked in anguish. "Why? Why now? Why me?"

"Because it is our destiny, my son, and this time it has fallen upon you," his father answered quietly. "It has been our family curse for generations. A malady which strikes the seventh son of a seventh son. When we were fortunate and a generation was spared, we dared to hope that the curse had at last run its course. But each time a seventh son begat a seventh son, the old fear, the dread, would return, often along with the reason for it all. Vanpir! All our hopes, our prayers, were of no avail. I'm sorry, Friedrich," his father had told him, "on my life, I would have spared you this agony, as I myself was spared; but I was weak, and could not compound this dreadful fate with blasphemy. I could not take your life, Friedrich, my dear son; I could not. And because I was weak, you are condemned to bear this bitter cross. I am so very sorry, my son. Try to forgive me."

"But, father, what shall I do? What will happen to me?"

It was Johan who replied. "You are not alone, Friedrich. There are others who are known to us. They shall soon be known to you. But you cannot stay here. You must come with me, to be sheltered and educated by the church. In spite of your affliction, you must make your way in the world. We can help you take your place among others like yourself. You can live, Friedrich. You must live—you have no choice."

And so Friedrich entered the walled enclave of the church, where he was shielded from the company of those he came to know only as "the others," and where he was educated in language, philosophy, history, and mathematics. Equally as important, he was taught to understand and control the awful powers his condition conferred, to avoid attention whenever he could, except among the protective association of their network, and to turn from the destructive, murderous actions that had previously marked his kind to acceptance of a gentler, more passive, path to obtaining the life force he needed.

When this education was complete, he was sent to join that connection and its minions in America, where he would henceforth live as he could among them, forever sheltered, his secret secure. He would enter a conspiracy, a necessary one, of a worldwide underground operating in the shadows, on the fringes and yet part of the wider society. An underground known as *In Sanguine Foedus*, Latin for 'a covenant ratified in blood,' but known simply, by its members and their minions, as the Network.

* * *

The air conditioner droned on in defense of the sauna-like weather outside Jordan's small second-floor apartment. The sun had been down for several hours, and the evening was in full blackout as he lazily shifted his body in the bed, stretching languorously before rolling over and curling into a fetal position, rebelling, as he always did, against the need to get up at all. It had been much the same routine for most of the two hundred and seventy-some years that he could remember of his life.

Still, he had to get up sometime, and he reluctantly began to mobilize for his coming shift with a quick review of the network's online notices, fortified with a cup of coffee and a couple of pieces of raisin toast. Immediately a red-flagged bulletin caught his attention and stopped him cold. It said, cryptically, "Big R blew doors off. Bird dogged by full grown bear."

The seemingly innocuous message was anything but that. The language was a variation of the lingo employed by truckers, so anyone accidentally coming across the network's communications would never be the wiser. Today's message, to an outsider familiar with CB chatter, simply meant that a Roadway Express truck had sped past a highway patrol cruiser equipped with a radar detector.

To Jordan and the other members of the forum, however, the passage carried a dire announcement: Someone in their network had gone rogue and was marked for extermination by the Shield, the organization's enforcement arm, and, when necessary, death squad. The bulletin was a chilling warning to them all of the dangers of crossing the line between passive ingestion of the blood energy they required for sustenance, and the more active practice of seeking to satisfy their needs with living victims.

Those crossing the line could not be tolerated, for their apprehension could expose the entire network to persecution. Rather, those errant members were hunted down and dispatched as only their kind could be: Either consumed by combustion; or by piercing the heart with a wooden stake, separating the head from the body, and cremating the remains.

As Jordan considered this latest news, his reverie was interrupted by the soft ping of his cell phone. It was his friend, Leandra, checking in before the start of her eight-to-four-night shift at Harborside Veterinary Hospital, a network enterprise.

"Hi, Jordan," she began. "I was just wondering if you'd seen today's flash."

"Yeah, Lee, just now. Is there any more information?"

"Not officially, but the scuttlebutt I hear is that the party in question has left the area. Smart move, although it won't help for long. No one has ever evaded apprehension. I suppose that's comforting, in a way, although it doesn't pay to dwell on how these things inevitably turn out."

"That's for sure," he agreed.

"Well, keep your eyes and ears open on this one; call me if you hear anything. I'll do the same."

"Okay, will do. Thanks. So long, Lee."

But Jordan couldn't shake the pall the bulletin had cast over the start of his evening, nor the feeling of sympathy he felt in spite of himself for the poor devil on the Shield's radar, or the unsettling knowledge that *there but for the grace of God go I.*

Once he had been one of the outsiders and their sunlit world, and he would have been as terrified and repulsed as they are now by what he had become, if they only knew.

His life then, what he remembered of it, had been ordinary enough—school, home, and apprenticing with his father to learn the trade passed down to him as it had been passed down to his father from his father, the practice going back four generations that they could account for; beyond that the lineage was murky and uncertain. He was to be a tailor; he understood that, and had accepted it. But a change was brewing, a greater plan for his life that came to fruition in his thirteenth year.

It seems so long ago, he thought, and of course it was. But the years passed quickly once the symptoms appeared and Jordan experienced the changes which caused him to shun contact with all but his parents, who alone shielded him in the beginning.

It had started with sleep disturbances, only mildly annoying at first, but gradually descending into episodes of devilish dreams; he would move about while still in the deep enthralls of twilight slumber, during which he would leave the house, only to return in the early dawn with his feet raw, his body and clothing smeared with blood, none of which he could account for. And there was the exhaustion, complete and debilitating, which drained his energy due to his lack of sleep and nightly forays to he knew not where.

His weight dropped precipitously, as the sight of food became suddenly and inexplicably repugnant to him. He became belligerent, increasingly nervous and irritable, unwilling to leave the house during the day, complaining that the sun's rays burned painfully when they fell upon his pale skin.

Only his father recognized the signs he had prayed would not befall his son, but his prayers went unanswered. When the signs could no longer be ignored, he knew he must prepare the boy to face his destiny, an unspeakable damnation that had afflicted the family throughout its long history, thankfully sparing some generations, then reappearing in others.

His older brother, Johan, had joined the church as soon as he became of age; it was to him that Jordan's father had turned, and so it was Johan who came to their house that long ago evening in early fall. The three of them had sat at the big table in the great workroom and Jordan listened as the other two spoke of the strange malady which had befallen him. One word appeared over and over during their discussion: Vanpir!

Friedrich has long since become Jordan Hoffmann, employed by Mr. Edgar Morton, director of the Ravenore Mortuary, one of a national chain controlled and operated by the network. The mortuary is located just off Lombard Street, in the Central district of South Baltimore, in the state of Maryland, one of the original thirteen colonies of the United States. Each morning, before dawn, Jordan returns to his second-floor apartment in the Old District, in a building operated by a landlady who asks no questions as long as the rent appears on time.

The apartment, in a neat row house on a block of neat row houses, is pleasant enough; he can't complain. But then, he never complains, for one domicile is like any other; his needs are met. This one is small, and sparsely furnished with no more than he needs; there are no pictures, mirrors, or trinkets taking up space either on the walls or on the top of the lone table beside his only window.

The view is meager as well; its focal point is an alley across the street, a kind of hobo jungle, with human traffic bearing sheets of cardboard; some struggle behind carts from a nearby market, overflowing with clothing and items randomly collected for cash or trade. Chilly nights are warmed by fires from makeshift heaters, and are busier than others, as people gather in the alley rather than camp in vacant spaces beside the harbor, or risk crime-and-disease-ridden shelters.

I could use a vacation, Jordan thought, with a hint of mirth at the very idea. Vacations were not for the likes of him. What communication, even camaraderie, he was able to enjoy with those others he knew to exist was possible only through their online forum—the actual blogs that existed to keep them connected, full of code words and innocent titles and themes to shield them from the prying eyes of outsiders, all carrying a double meaning they alone could decode.

But they knew who they were. They met from time to time to reinforce their bond, and they were more numerous than the outer world could ever suspect. They were the revenants, the living dead, and they spoke, and planned, and shared their dreams much as did those who moved about in the sunlit world; but that was all they had in common.

* * *

Jordan's job, in a section of the city where recent renovation had replaced a number of formerly-decaying warehouses and factories, was bearable enough, even pleasant, in that it gave him time to read, and Mr. Morton didn't mind the time he spent corresponding over the network, as long as his work was finished and the workrooms were in order before he left. That work depended on the schedule of visitations, funerals, and cremations to take place the following day. In preparation for such scheduling, Jordan charted the incoming bodies and began the preliminary steps if embalming was to take place. This involved removing any clothing or jewelry and detailing any marks on the body, which would then be shaved and positioned as it would be when placed in the casket for viewing. Then he injected embalming fluid into an artery while simultaneously draining any blood from a nearby vein or from the heart.

At this point, Mr. Morton or his assistant took over and completed the process up to the last step, when make-up was applied and the body was made presentable for viewing, in which case Jordan or another technician applied those finishing touches.

In the course of his duties, Jordan was able to access a necessary source of nourishment, an energy elixir which would flow through his veins to keep his body animated and limit the damage of decay, an elixir which otherwise would go to waste when it drained into the sewer beneath the establishment.

The mortuary was within walking distance of Jordan's apartment. It wasn't an easy walk—about two miles each way—but he relished the usually-deserted streets and the time it gave him to think.

The night before, he had been stopped by a police cruiser as he hurried along, hugging the shadowy buildings. When they pulled to the curb just ahead of him, he paused to address the two shadowy figures inside the darkened vehicle.

"Good evening, officers," he said. "Can I help you?" he asked from the middle of the sidewalk. He tried to speak first whenever these confrontations occurred, hoping the tactic would defuse any tension inherent in a potentially dangerous situation on both sides.

The officer nearest him rolled down the window. "Good evening, sir. Kind of late to be out here. Mind if we ask what you're doing in this neighborhood?"

"Not at all. I'm on my way home from work."

"Do you have some identification?"

Jordan handed over his identification card, which was duly scrutinized.

"Mind telling us where you work?"

"Ravenore Mortuary. You can call to verify that if you like. Mr. Morton should still be there."

The mention of the mortuary and Jordan's invitation to have his employer vouch for him satisfied their curiosity. Plus the thought of calling a funeral home at two in the morning wasn't the way they wanted to end their shift. Besides, who would come up with that story if it weren't true and could be so easily verified?

Handing back Jordan's card, the officer said, "Thank you, Mr. Hoffman. I don't think that will be necessary. Have a good night, but watch yourself on these streets; they can be pretty mean."

"I'll be careful. Thank you for stopping."

The window slowly closed and the cruiser ambled away from the curb to continue up the block, turning right at the corner. Jordan continued walking. When he crossed the street where the cruiser had turned off, there was no sign of it. He wondered who had really stopped him, and why. Was it just a routine patrol stopping a suspicious character on a deserted street? Or were they part of the Shield's surveillance squad, on alert for the network rogue? He didn't know, but he walked a little faster.

* * *

One early morning, in the twilight between night and breaking dawn, Jordan returned to his apartment after his shift. He was fixing a snack when his phone rang. It was James, the network's programmer.

"Did you see the bulletin?" James began abruptly.

Jordan guessed he was referring to the earlier alert.

"Yes. Do they know who?"

"They do now. The name has just been released. Jordan, it's Cam Hollister."

James pronounced the name slowly and distinctly, aware of the impact it would have on his friend. And he was right—it was a name Jordan had hoped never to hear, because he knew Cam. He also knew how the saga would end—the only way it could: Cam would die.

"There's no doubt?" Jordan asked.

"No. It's definite. He was seen and identified, and now he's on the run."

"Any idea where he'll head?"

"No. But how far can he go without help? No one in the network will lift a finger for him. He may as well turn himself in and get it over with. Now or later, it'll end the same."

"Man, I feel bad about this," Jordan said. "Any idea what turned him?"

"Nada. But I doubt he just cracked. Everyone I've talked to is surprised as hell, and no one seemed to have any idea it was happening. I don't know how it could have been missed, but that's what they say."

"How bad is it?"

"Now that the story is coming out, it apparently started with animals, the usual way. Mutilation. At first the discoveries were written off as a cult doing its thing; I guess that's why no one connected the dots. Weird rites, something like that; at least that's how he tried to make it appear. They would have stopped him for that alone, but it took a while for a pattern to show up. Now there's no doubt. He's turned and been spotted. Three dead for sure, maybe more."

"There's no hope then?"

"No, Jordan. Not now. No way. It's too late and gone too far. I just wanted to let you know in case he shows up at your place. They know you two were friends, so they think he may try to get your help. Don't do it, Jordan. Just a warning, pal. You could be under surveillance already. There's a real manhunt underway, and it's serious."

The prospect of being in the crosshairs of the Shield sent a chill through Jordan's body. He knew little of their actual operation, but had heard enough stories of their deadly efficiency to know that attracting their attention in any form was to be avoided if at all possible.

"Well, I haven't seen him for months," he said, suddenly wary, choosing his words, even with someone he considered a friend, "so it's not likely he'd show up here. He's probably holed up somewhere, maybe already hopped a freight or stowed away in some hold." Jordan wondered why he hoped James believed that.

"There's nowhere he can go, not for long. There'll be a trail now, and they'll track him. He has to know that." *What was James really telling him? That a trap is closing on his former friend? A trap that could ensnare him too?*

"Yeah."

"Well, anyway, just so you know."

"Yeah, James. Thanks for calling."

Jordan prepared his meal and thought about their conversation. He knew immediately James was referring to the rogue in the network bulletin. *But Cam. Oh, gee...not Cam.*

He had met Cam Hollister shortly after arriving in Baltimore several years before. They became friends and for a while were inseparable. Cam had been Jordan's guide to the city, and introduced him to others in the network who lived and worked in the harbor district or nearby, and pointed out the safe houses any one of them could go to in case of trouble on the street.

But gradually he and Cam drifted apart; Jordan never quite knew why. Now he suspected that Cam, even then, was beginning to feel the stirrings that would eventually make him dissatisfied with passively-obtained nutrients, and he might have already begun to seek out live prey. From what James had said, Cam had started with animal kills that he disguised as cult rituals—mutilating the carcasses, removing and scattering the entrails. Anyone finding the remains might not realize the real point to the killings was the blood lust that had become, for Cam, irresistible.

And James thought Jordan himself was possibly being watched. *If so, could they have tapped his phone, too? No, that's just paranoid.* Jordan reassured himself he had nothing to fear from the Shield; in fact, he hoped they *were* watching him. If Cam did try to contact him, or maybe just showed up somewhere in the area, they might intercept him before he got to Jordan, and that would be just as well, because there was nothing Jordan could, or dared, do to help his friend without engineering his own destruction in the process.

* * *

Over the many long and lonely years, Jordan had, from time to time, entered relationships beyond the network when the solitariness of his nocturnal existence seemed too much to bear. It never ended well. He did not age, his companions did. At some point, if the relationship continued, they began to wonder, to ask questions he dared not answer. Often he would simply walk away, other times he would try to explain his situation as a genetic condition called Syndrome X, the opposite of the rapid-aging condition known as progeria. This was accepted up to a point, and then the wondering and questioning would begin again, especially when his companions began to exhibit the effects of aging while he remained ever young.

In those very rare instances when his connection with an outsider was too strong to bear walking away, Jordan remained steadfast while his companion experienced the stages of a natural lifetime, explaining their relationship in various ways as the years passed through a normal life cycle—lover, friend, relative, guardian—until the other's end time came.

* * *

Moonlight reflected off the Bay as water sloshed rhythmically against the wharf. It was near midnight, and the four members of the squad had gathered beside the marina hangar to compare notes on the hunt.

Walter Cummings, area security supervisor, began: "What's the latest?" he asked, scanning the faces of the other members of his crew.

"We're closing in," Frank Tomachek replied. "We know he's somewhere in the District. We're searching every building, street, and alleyway right now. It can't be long. We'll get him, maybe tonight."

"Let's hope so," his chief replied. "He's been out too long already. He's got to be getting help to have made it this far, and we may have a sympathizer to deal with as well as the rogue. It doesn't look good. We need to put this one to bed soon."

"We will, sir," Tomachek assured him.

* * *

It was a few weeks after the conversation with James that a gang rumble on a particularly sultry summer evening resulted in a larger-than-usual number of weekend casualties, and many of the neighborhood families of those involved chose Mr. Morton's establishment for the final arrangements.

Jordan extended his hours as much as he dared, and returned to his apartment after a particularly grueling shift. As he let himself in, he reached around the jamb for the light switch and flicked it up. Nothing happened.

Now what? he thought. *Fuse blown? Bulb burned out?* Then he realized the ceiling fixture controlled by the switch had four bulbs; it was unlikely all had gone bad. *Still, the lights were on in the hallway, and that fuse controlled the power for his section of the second floor, so it couldn't be a fuse.*

Then his breath caught as he realized it wasn't a fuse. *Someone had turned out the bulbs in the fixture controlled by the wall switch.* There was only one person he could think of likely to be waiting for him in the darkened room.

"Cam?" he whispered hoarsely.

"Yeah. Close the door," came the hushed reply.

Jordan stepped inside and closed the door. Standing in the darkness, he wondered what to expect.

"Can I turn a lamp on?" he asked.

"Okay." The voice was close, somewhere to his left.

Jordan felt his way to the sofa and used it as a guide to feel his way to the end table beside it. He found the lamp and turned the knob. The light was softly dim, but bright enough. He turned around to face his visitor, and involuntarily recoiled at the sight.

Cam had been standing against the wall beside the door, and remained there after the light came on. But Jordan hardly recognized him.

"Cam? What the...,"

The creature standing beside the closed door looked like a fugitive from the grave. His eyes were bloodshot, his hair was matted, and his skin was the color of the cadavers Jordan worked on, except that this one wasn't on a slab in a refrigerated vault, it was here in his room, facing him.

"Cam, what are you doing here? They're looking for you. You know you can't hide much longer. Even I may be watched right now. I can't help you, you know that. As much as I might want to, I can't."

"I know, Jordan. I know, but I'm just so very tired. I can't run any more. There's no place left to go. Could I stay here just a little while? Just a little while, that's all, and then I'll go, and you'll never see me again. I swear."

Jordan knew he couldn't refuse. "I'll make some coffee," he said at last. "You hungry?"

Cam laughed. It was a sick, smirking, evil laugh that made Jordan wish he had never come home.

"You know what I mean," he said.

"Yeah. But it's been a while. I almost forgot."

"Well, do you want me to fix you a burger? I have some buns and patties in the freezer; it won't take long."

"Yeah, Jordan. That would be nice. Thanks."

"No problem. Sit down at the table. It'll be just a minute."

Jordan heated the water for the coffee and brought out a hamburger bun and cooked patty with onions. He had made a batch over the weekend and froze most of them.

The teakettle whistled just as the microwave bell went off, signaling the burger was thawed and heated enough to eat. Jordan fixed the coffee with cream and sugar, the way he remembered Cam liked it, and set it and the food before his visitor. He got some coffee for himself and took his seat across the table so they could talk.

He waited awhile as Cam demolished the burger and then sat back, running his finger around the rim of his cup, over and over.

Finally, Jordan said, "What happened, Cam?"

The thing that had been his friend remained silent for a time. When it finally began to speak, it told a familiar story, one Jordan had heard many times over the centuries, but never from someone he had been so close to.

"I just don't know, Jordan. I honestly don't," the story began as they often did. "I thought I was on an even keel, and that I could get along like you and the others in the network; for a long time I did. And then it all just fell apart. The stirrings...you know? At first I tried to ignore them, distract myself. But it was no good. Then I told myself just a little...something small...maybe just once in a while...and then I'd be okay, I'd be able to handle it."

"It doesn't work that way, Cam. You can never, ever start. Not small, not at all. Never."

"I soon found that out. But by then it was too late. I'd read about ritual animal sacrifice, so I tried to make it look like that, maybe the work of some voodoo practice or something. It seemed to work for a while, just not very long. All too soon it wasn't enough. Not nearly enough. The urge got stronger and stronger; I felt like I would explode if I didn't find some release. And so it started, and I swear to you that I couldn't help myself. I couldn't, Jordan; I just couldn't. The first was a tramp in the railroad yard. Jordan, you can't know what it feels like, or I swear you wouldn't be able to do it any other way. It's the way we were meant to be, not this off-the-shelf crap, but the real thing—warm, flowing. Oh, man, it felt so good."

"You have to go now, Cam. You know that," Jordan reminded him coldly.

His long-ago friend sighed. "Yeah, I know," he said softly.

Jordan wondered if Cam would leave peacefully, and watched him slowly rise and make his way to the door. They were evenly matched, if it came to that, but Jordan didn't want to risk a scratch or bite that might send him down the same road Cam was now traveling. Things were already hard enough.

With his hand on the knob, Cam turned and said quietly, "Try to remember me as I used to be. Can you do that?"

"Yes, Cam. It's the only way I'll ever think of you."

"Thank you. Goodbye now. Take care."

"You, too."

Cam turned the knob, opened the door, and silently slipped through it. Jordan cautiously crossed the room, closed and locked the door, and wondered what would happen next, how the end would come. He felt helpless, useless, but also relieved. He was out of it now; the fates would take their course.

He stood for a while, sadly thinking through this last meeting. Then he began to clear the table. He was about to wash the few dishes when he heard the muted fadeout of a siren's wail. It was close, very close—from the street in front of his building. *Could they have found Cam?* Maybe.

He knew the Shield had members on the police force; it was a common cover. He went to the window and looked down at the street. What he saw there held him spellbound in horror, unable to turn away.

The siren had indeed come for Cam, who was standing at the entrance to the alley across the street, on a pile of cardboard, rags, and other debris which he had gathered and soaked in gasoline.

Cam, his friend, who had been unable to resist a destructive road with no exit, was standing there engulfed in flames, looking up at Jordan's window.

The officers who responded parked their cruisers and stood around the awful conflagration.

"It's over," Cummings murmured, noting Cam's gaze toward Jordan's figure in the second story window across the street. He and his crew bore silent witness to the end, when they retrieved Cam's remains, cleared the residue of the blaze until no trace was left, and simply melted away.

It was some time until Jordan was able to leave the window and the awful sight he would never forget. He turned out the lights in the apartment and sat on the sofa, thinking...about Cam...about James and Leandra...about himself...until the morning's glow intensified and threatened to spread throughout the room. But mostly he thought about Cam, who would ultimately be no more than another blip on the screen of the endless feature that was his existence.

He got up then, secured the night shades, drew the heavily-lined draperies so they overlapped and no light penetrated any crevice in the apartment, and he went to bed.

The next evening Jordan roused himself with a strange sense of relief. The millstone that had been his association with Cam had been lifted from his shoulders, although it bothered him that he should think of their friendship that way. Yet, surprisingly, he found himself looking forward to the start of his shift. Perhaps the thought of the well-stocked shelves in Mr. Morton's basement storeroom had something to do with his feeling of unusual contentment. He didn't know. He only knew that long after the shadow of evening hours had obliterated all trace of the afternoon's fading light, and the hands of the clock on the nightstand inexorably reached the appointed hour, he would once again rise to begin a new segment of a life that stretched to infinity.

- The End -

- The Last Cookie -

Darkness is closing in on our cozy neighborhood at the edge of a small Midwestern city. Soon the denizens of the night will be out and about, and for the past few years our two-story cream brick house on Bascar Lane has been one of numerous stops on their nightly search for food.

"Do you think they'll come tonight?" my husband, Bill, asked me.

"I'm sure something will," I replied. "Sooner or later, something will surely show up."

We had purchased the house on Bascar Lane about three years before. It had everything we were looking for: the deck, extra bedrooms, dining room, and full basement I wanted; and the fireplace, fenced yard, and pine trees Bill looked for. It didn't seem possible that one property could combine it all, and I was especially skeptical when Bill threw in the part about the pine trees. So when we saw the older house on the large corner lot, with its rear deck, fenced yard, and several large pine trees dotting the property, we knew we had found our new home.

Bill and I are both animal lovers, and at a previous property we had lived with a German shepherd for many years, until old age made her life difficult, and we faced the agonizing but inevitable decision every pet owner dreads. We went through a lot with that animal because we loved her, but memories of that experience caused us to be torn as to repeating it. We ultimately decided that we would not have a pet once we retired and moved to the house we had always wanted, with the amenities we had always wished for.

But while we thought we had lost our enthusiasm for pets and were through with animals, we soon found that they were not through with us, for our little urban haven teemed with birds, squirrels, rabbits, and chipmunks. It didn't take long before Bill put up feeders, houses, and water dishes. We even received official recognition of our property as a natural wildlife habitat. The sign announcing it as such became a gathering place for the various creatures that visited for the seeds, nuts, and fruit we offered. Two bird baths and three additional ground pans of water all got their share of local traffic.

And that was just the daytime crowd. After a while, we became aware of nighttime visitors, too. I don't remember which came first, but soon we had regular sightings of raccoons; occasionally a possum or skunk would drop by; and periodically we'd see a fox in the early morning hours, scrambling about the street, but never on our property; of course, it may have found its way under the fence when we weren't looking, just as the other animals did. All were drawn by the fresh water we kept available in pans Bill cleaned daily.

It wasn't long before we began putting out bits of food we had saved for the nighttime crowd, just samplings of fruit at first, although we were always on the lookout for the vermin that would have shut down those offerings if they ever appeared.

Bill is a natural nurturer, and at a previous home had set up a feeding station for the birds right outside our bedroom window. We enjoyed watching their antics, until one evening I looked out to find a mouse helping himself to the seed. Soon after we had such an infestation of our garage (they even made a nest in the tangled tubing of our car's engine compartment) that the feeding program was ruined. We stopped cold and evicted the unwanted visitors.

The initial problem that arose on Bascar Lane wasn't mice, however, and thank goodness we never saw the larger version. No, the problem we encountered was with squirrels gnawing at the openings of Bill's bird houses. He put metal flanges around the openings to discourage them, and for a while it did; but then they began to gnaw at other parts of the houses, determined to get at the eggs or little ones inside. When we couldn't protect the birds, we dismantled the feeders and took the houses down. Fortunately, a neighbor had several feeders which he tended regularly, so we contented ourselves with the birds eating there and coming to us for water.

When winter came, we worried about the animals. How could they forage when the ground was frozen and snow covered? That was when we decided to find some way to help them through the season. Our original intent was just to provide a little nourishment during the worst of the winter months, intending to force them to fend for themselves once spring came and the ground thawed; we never intended the year-round feeding program our efforts spawned.

After mulling over and discarding any number of possibilities, we decided on dog food. After a bit of trial and error, we settled on a brand that advertised "tender morsels." We bought huge sacks of the stuff, which usually lasted a couple of weeks; it was a huge hit. The raccoons, and everything else that we could occasionally glimpse, took to it as if they were raised on it. The standard portion became three heaping bowls, either pie plates or whipped topping containers, each crowned with a cookie of some sort, usually whatever happened to be on sale that week at the supermarket.

Sometimes, if it snowed, nothing would come for the food, and it would be untouched in the morning. "The animals are staying put, afraid of being tracked in the fresh snow," Bill suggested. That might be, but when several days went by with the dishes untouched, I did a bit of research and found out that while raccoons, in particular, don't hibernate as such, they do go into some kind of a light sleep, and will only venture out from time to time during winter.

One night, I believe it was in late May, the raccoons had come and gone early and that night's food bowls were empty. It was around ten-thirty, and we were on our way up to bed, when we heard a thumping noise coming from the deck. We put the outside light on and opened the draperies to see the source of the disturbance. It was a mother raccoon with four small kits swarming over her; she was trying to pry open the screen door. We soon realized she had come for something to eat and found the buffet closed. With her brood, she was desperate, and was doing all she could to find food—by appealing to the humans she must have realized were the source of the offerings she had come to depend on. Out came refills for the food bowls and a second round of cookies. For us it was a memorable exercise in interspecies communication, a request we were happy to oblige.

Providing the night-roaming animals with scraps of food to supplement the dog food worked well for a long time, and was a useful outlet for the occasional overripe grapes, pears, peaches, bits of fat and gravy that might otherwise have gone to waste. They became accustomed to checking for food on the bricks beneath our kitchen window, and it wasn't long before we caught a glimpse of something or other chowing down on the offering of the night. The bowls would go out after dark, and an hour later were licked so clean they looked as if they had been washed. Our customers gathered under the deck and waited until they heard Bill set out the evening's fare. Many times he was unable to return to the living room before the bowls would be in the process of having their contents demolished. That done, the visitors went on their way, having learned there were seldom seconds.

When the animals squabbled over the single bowl we originally provided, we divided the treat between two bowls. That helped, but not for long. Soon that too was not enough, and the squabbles became more vicious; it seems there were two bowls, but three raccoons—that we saw.

We thought the disputes were over when we added a third bowl and, again, for a while, peace reigned. Three bowls, three raccoons. Then, one night, we were horrified when we turned on the light to discover a squirming horde of raccoons climbing in and out and over the three bowls. We counted fifteen in all, and couldn't be sure that was the entire pack. But it was a wakeup call to be sure.

We had largely managed to hide our feeding station from the surrounding neighbors, who may have suspected what was going on, but couldn't know for sure, as the bowls went out after dark, were largely shielded by shrubbery, and were picked up at dawn. But the sheer size of the horde that descended that night made us realize that it wouldn't go unnoticed much longer.

Our neighbors are good people, but we had heard comments about what mean, vicious, dangerous animals raccoons were. That description did not fit the animals that came to our house looking for handouts. It would not have been difficult to make pets out of any number of them in the years they came to our yard. One in particular was Bill's favorite, and I have to admit even I thought he was special; we, of course, assumed it was a 'he.'

This particular animal was part of a small group that came to the feeding station one night. When Bill, balancing the food bowls, opened the patio door, they all ran for cover except one; he boldly ran to Bill, pushing against his leg as if urging him to be quicker with the food, so Bill named him Charger.

Charger had learned that if he got a cookie and took it under the deck to eat, he would be swamped by the others who were also eager for the treat. It wasn't long before Charger managed to arrive before the others; he would sit on the patio and look through the door, entranced by the TV screen, until we noticed him. When we put the food out, he hastily retrieved a cookie and ran to a corner of the deck in an attempt to eat it in peace.

After a while, I tried hand feeding him, and quickly created a monster. Charger began to claw at the door to the deck to get our attention, and sometimes he was not alone. Many a night I stood at the outer door and cracked it open just enough to get my hand through with a cookie. Charger lunged for the cookie while muscling his companion out of the way; his claws sometimes scraped my hand—they felt like needles being dragged lightly across my skin. Charger would snatch the cookie and run to a corner of the deck, where a squabble would ensue as his companion tried to wrest it away from him. After watching these antics, I soon kept two cookies handy, one for Charger and the other to throw on the deck to distract his companion. Their preoccupation with their cookies was such that I have no doubt they would have come right in the house with very little encouragement. The cookie prize was serious business indeed!

After that, as soon as we opened the patio door, Charger tried to force his way inside, and we had to physically force him back. But one thing that impressed Bill most of all, and which he constantly commented on, was how gentle and polite Charger was when taking his cookie from Bill's hand. And if Bill placed his hand against the inside of the glass door, Charger would move his paw to match Bill's hand placement.

The last time we saw Charger was five in the morning on the first day of our vacation. Bill had gone to the garage entry door on his way to collect the previous evening's dishes, and he couldn't get the door open. Charger was outside, braced against the door; he had apparently been waiting for Bill to come out. Bill said he didn't know why Charger was waiting for him there, because Bill had never come out that way with the food bowls. That morning, Charger got two cookies for his efforts.

We left on our vacation and were gone a week. We never saw Charger again.

We still miss our little friend and wonder why he never returned; his actions were so distinctive, we would have recognized him among all the animals that frequented the feeding area since then.

We enjoyed Charger's antics and miss them; when he stopped coming, we never knew why. We had heard that someone else in the neighborhood was feeding the raccoons and even allowing them in their garage. Still, we couldn't imagine Charger doing without his cookies; but we never really knew why he just seemed to disappear.

Bill and I had been reluctant to act regarding the raccoon situation. We had discussed trying to trap and relocate them to a nearby wildlife area, but wanted to be certain we did not separate a mother from little ones who still depended on her. And so we coasted and did nothing as that final winter turned to spring and melded into early summer.

One day a neighbor mentioned to Bill that he had been finding "presents" in his yard; he blamed the raccoons and said that a friend was bringing a trap over and would trap the raccoons while the neighbor was on vacation. Further conversation revealed that the friend was a licensed trapper who planned to trap the animals and turn them in for a bounty on their pelts.

Trap...bounty...pelts?

We thought it was just talk until a trap appeared on the neighbor's lawn early one morning—with a panicked little raccoon trying desperately to find a way out.

Trap...bounty...pelts?

Bill slipped over and freed the little guy that time, but then we knew we could wait no longer; we had to act.

Bill's own trap went out that night. The animals weren't used to anything but bowls in their feeding area, so it wasn't long before the trap had served its purpose, although not without a little fine tuning. Somehow the first raccoon to encounter it had managed to avoid stepping on the trigger and made off with the dog food we had used for bait. I suggested we tie a cookie to the back of the cage. When the raccoon had to tug at the cookie, he would have to step on the trigger. It worked.

That raccoon was the vanguard that others would soon follow. Bill loaded the trap in the bed of his pickup and drove out to the wildlife area. When he returned, he said he had picked a good spot beside a stream that crisscrossed the woods. When he mentioned that the raccoon had eaten the cookie on the way over, I told him, "It might well be the last cookie he ever enjoys, unless he happens on some campers' leftovers."

After that early success, the trap went out nightly until it was too late for trips to the relocation area; then Bill brought it in and set out the food bowls so the animals would continue to come.

Since the first capture and relocation, there have been almost two dozen more, all adult and half grown raccoons, and all released in the same spot; hopefully, they will find one another and finally make their way in the wild as they were intended to live. Through it all, Bill has commented often that he is amazed how none of the animals ever showed any hostility toward him. They were docile in the trap, never snarling, biting, or clawing at Bill all the while they were collected and transported. Once they were at their destination and Bill opened the trap door, they simply scampered off into the woods. I've often wondered if they realized what was happening, that we did what we did to save their lives and help them to live free in the forest as they were meant to, and not confined in an urban jungle maze.

"Once they stop coming for the food and no more are found in the trap, I'm going to stop feeding them," Bill announced. He added, "Well, maybe I'll put something out this winter just to help them through, and next year we'll see what the situation looks like."

- The End –

- Jaded -

As his gaze wandered over the decrepit furnishings of the hole-in-the-wall that served as his office, Phil Newland was irritated by the layer of recalcitrant dust that persisted in making itself at home on every visible surface. *Something has to be done,* he thought, *and now.* Whereupon he rose and closed the blinds that covered most of the single window in the room, thus preventing the sun from reminding him of the fact that his janitorial service had decided to avoid his suite until he paid the bill which had somehow become three months delinquent.

Something has to break, he told himself, or one day soon he would arrive at his office to find the lock on his door had been changed and his belongings neatly stacked outside in the hall.

Looking through the previous day's paper for the third time, Phil heard something in his outer office. *Were they shutting him down already?* The thought passed when he heard a woman's voice call, "Mr. Newland? Hello? Is anyone here?"

Roused by the sudden prospect of business, Phil jumped to his feet and made his way to the door, hitting his hip on the edge of his desk as he tripped over his wastebasket, which had not been emptied anytime during the previous week.

Reaching the closed door with the frosted glass bearing his name over the words, <u>Private Investigation</u>, he took a deep breath to compose himself. Then he opened the door and walked through.

Standing in the middle of the room beside what had been his secretary's desk, before the last girl he hired abruptly quit after mumbling something about a bounced check, was a rather nice-looking woman Phil guessed to be in her mid-to-late thirties, one whom he had never seen before. She had dark, shoulder length hair and was conservatively dressed in a dark blue wool suit with some kind of piping outlining the collar. His eyes gravitated to her left hand—no wedding ring. He wondered what she wanted, as he had not advertised for a replacement for his previous assistant.

"I'm Phil Newland. May I help you?" he offered.

"Well, I hope you will indeed help me," she said. "I very much need your help in finding something extremely valuable."

It took a minute before Phil realized he was face to face with a potential client.

"I see," he said, playing for time while he collected his thoughts. "I'm afraid my girl is not in today—sitter trouble. Why don't you come into my office and let me know what I can do for you?"

The woman looked over the desk beside her, taking in the obsolete computer monitor and the keyboard with the brown stain splashed across the keys. Recognizing neglect well over a day old, she hesitated. Finally deciding that as long as she was in the office she may as well talk to the man, she moved toward him, all the while appraising the detective she was looking to for help.

The man was about her own age; she was surprised that he was not taller, for he was nearly her own height. His hair was dark and curly, and in need of a trim. He wore glasses, which gave him a rather bookish look. Sam Spade? Mike Hammer? No.

Phil showed her to an empty chair across the desk from his own, and was glad he had closed the blinds. The sun peeking around the edges and the single fluorescent light overhead provided all the illumination they needed.

Seating herself tentatively in the chair, the woman unconsciously sniffed the air. Recognizing the odor as something either dead or rotten, she wished she were still in the outer hall. Suddenly she heard a voice say, "May I have your name, Miss?"

Reminded of where she was and what had brought her there, she said, "Yes, of course, Mr. Newland. Please forgive me. I have a great deal on my mind just now."

"That's quite all right. But please tell me your name and how I may be of service to you."

In spite of her initial trepidation, Phil's friendliness and apparent willingness to help her caused her prior reserve to soften, and she began to tell her story.

"My name is Georgia Redfield," she began. "I work for the Worthington Gallery as an appraiser of antiques, particularly Ming dynasty jade."

"I see," Phil said, his interest piqued by the mention of antique jade. He was beginning to see dollar signs occupying his visitor's chair.

"And what brought you to me?" He wondered who could have made the referral, and what he could have done to impress them enough to recommend him.

"Well, the gallery is just up the street from your office. I see your name on the window when I wait for the bus on my way home."

"Oh." So much for satisfied clients. "Well, now that I know your name and how you found me, perhaps you could tell me just what it is that makes you feel you need the services of a private investigator."

And so she began. "I believe a very valuable jade vase has been stolen and replaced with a cheap imitation. But now I'm suspected of authenticating the replacement to hide the switch. It's not true, Mr. Newland. The piece I authenticated was genuine, I know it was; there is simply no way I could mistake a distinctive eighteenth century rose jade vase with what appears to be a plastic replica."

"I see," Phil said for the third time.

With this, she sat back and looked at him expectantly. A minute went by before he realized she was expecting him to say something. A minute during which he wondered just what he would say, should say, that would give her at least a little confidence that she had come to the right place and from whom she could expect some help, some encouragement that she would not be spending the best years of her life observing the world through prison bars.

As all this passed through Phil's mind, he knew he had to tell her something, he just didn't know what. Then, as if a lifeline were being thrown to him from another dimension, he heard himself say, "Miss Redfield, I need a bit more information, then I'd like you to leave the matter with me. There are several avenues I need to explore. I believe you were not mistaken in your appraisal. Someone has intervened to redirect a valuable item. I believe their efforts have left a trail which I intend to follow. Give me a few days to run down some leads. In the meantime, go about your business as usual; as soon as I have some information, I'll be in touch."

Phil was impressed with his little speech, which he hoped sounded convincing to his prospective client; that he didn't believe any of it he would keep to himself.

His speech, surprisingly, seemed to mollify Miss Redfield. She no longer appeared to be looking for an opportunity to bolt for the door. Instead, she said, "Very well, Mr. Newland. I'll do as you say and wait for your call. Thank you so much for seeing me and listening to my problem. For the first time since this happened I feel all may be well after all."

Phil was aware of their subsequent conversation during which he gathered the information he felt he would need to put together some kind of theory regarding just what could have happened to the item in question. He found out that her supervisor was the owner and manager of the gallery where she had been employed for ten years, Harvey Worthington. They also went over the procedure she followed in shipping the vase to the purchaser, a John Kandle in Baltimore. She had packed the vase herself and prepared it for shipping, then turned it over to the shipping department with instructions for insurance arrangements with the carrier, Apex Freight. "We have used Apex for years and there had never been a problem until this last shipment." Their agent came that afternoon to collect the package, and she was convinced that was the end of the matter. Three days later, Mr. Kandle called Mr. Worthington in a rage, demanding to know what kind of joke they thought they were playing. When Mr. Kandle calmed down enough to explain the situation, he said that when he received the package from Apex, he opened it immediately. Inside was a cheap pink plastic, he emphasized *plastic*, vase, hardly the rose jade vessel he had agreed to pay some twenty-six thousand dollars for.

When he heard the price, Phil felt a hard lump form in his throat. "Twenty-six thousand dollars?" he croaked. He had a sinking feeling he was in well over his head; this was looking like a job for the FBI, at least. Then he thought of his bills, and decided he would have a go at the caper first; if he failed, the Feds would still be there.

Miss Redfield explained just what made the item in question so valuable to a serious collector like Mr. Kandle. She looked at Phil, took a deep breath, exhaled, and began. "Well, to keep it simple, jade is considered a gemstone. While it is particularly meaningful to the Chinese people, it is valued in many cultures. It is particularly prized in the green form, although it appears in a half dozen other colors, all of which are considered valuable either in spite of, or because of, the color variance.

"The vase I appraised was a particularly fine Ming dynasty specimen in rose jade, known among the collecting community as the Rose Key. I inspected it, verified its provenance, and appraised it for twenty-five to thirty thousand dollars. The collector, Mr. Kandle, had already agreed upon a price of twenty-six thousand in a previous negotiation with Mr. Worthington. Actually, Mr. Worthington had been searching for such a piece on behalf of Mr. Kandle for the better part of a year before finally being alerted to its existence in a collection in San Francisco. The appraisal price is actually only on the legitimate market; there are unscrupulous collectors who would actually pay a great deal more because of the rarity of the coloration and striation inherent in the piece.

"Mr. Worthington went to San Francisco to negotiate with the collector there, who agreed to part with the piece. Mr. Worthington brought it back here with him and I verified its value. Mr. Newland, it was a beautiful piece with exquisite veining. We notified Mr. Kandle, wired him its provenance and pictures, and he agreed to wire the money upon receipt of the vase." At this point, she reached in her bag and retrieved a picture of the object in question.

Phil, whose knowledge of jade consisted only in knowing how to spell it, inspected the photo. It was certainly a handsome enough vase, even he could agree to that, although when he thought of the price tag attached to it, he realized it took an understanding far greater than his to fully appreciate the piece. He also didn't understand a lot of what she said; he figured he would just have to take her word for it.

They spent an hour while Phil gathered the information he felt he would need to pursue her case with any amount of intelligence. After once again assuring her he would do all he could to find the errant object, he walked her to the door and said, "Just one thing more, Miss Redfield."

"Yes?"

"Well, we may be in contact rather frequently before this is over, and I think it would be all right if you called me Phil."

Seemingly taken aback by this simple request, she smiled and said, "Thank you, Phil. And you may call me Georgia." Something about their little exchange made him smile, too.

Once again alone in his office, Phil opened the blinds and sat staring out the window, trying to gather his thoughts and decide on a course of action. The view was hardly inspiring as the only window in the office faced the brick wall of the building next door. However, a half hour of staring at the loose and missing mortar connecting the crumbling bricks in the sagging wall accomplished its purpose: Phil had an idea. He decided to touch base with his friend on the local constabulary, Sergeant Joe Rizzo, whom he met while he was bussing tables at the Imperial Dragon Chinese restaurant. Phil often did odd jobs in the kitchen when he was between cases and had time on his hands; the owner, Mr. Chi Ho Chan, was happy to trade a meal for a few hours of extra help.

Rizzo answered on the third ring. "Well, hello, Phil. How are you?"

"Hi, Joe. I'm fine, just fine. And yourself?"

"Could always be better. And now to what do I owe the pleasure this fine afternoon?"

"I just had a visitor. A Georgia Redfield from Worthington Gallery..."

"About the pink vase that got lost in transit?"

Phil felt stupid. He should have known that, of course, the gallery would have notified the police, and a theft of that amount would surely have come to Joe's attention.

"That's the one."

"The Redfield woman contacted you, not her boss?"

"Worthington probably figured he did all he had to when he notified you. But she insists there was no mistake in her appraisal. She says the vase was switched somewhere along the line, and I tend to agree with her."

"So you've taken the case?"

"Righto. I'm just touching base with you so maybe we could trade information, although right now I'm kind of short on chips since she just left my office."

"Well, Phil, I think we're starting out pretty much even. She packed up a pricy collectible and what arrived was a piece of junk."

"Yeah, that's about it," Phil agreed, wondering if he and the police would be watering the same plant. "What do you have so far, so I don't beat the same bush?"

"Not much chance of that, Phil. We just don't have the resources to go beating down doors in search of a flower pot that was insured to the gills."

"Insured? By the gallery?"

"No, the shipper—Apex."

There was a silence while Phil digested this bit of information. Then he said, "Whoa. Are you saying *Apex* guaranteed the shipment?"

"Yep. So you'd think if anyone had an incentive to find the vase, it would be Apex."

"Yeah, you'd think so, wouldn't you?" Phil just got a funny feeling, the feeling that came over him when something fishy was going on. He kept it to himself; no point in stirring the pot if it turned out to be a nothing there there.

"You smelling something not quite right?"

"I don't know yet, Joe. I think I'll nose around a bit. I'll let you know if I turn up something."

"Sounds good. Keep in touch."

"Will do. So long, Joe."

After hanging up, Phil thought about his relationship with his cop friend. He liked Rizzo, but worried about him, too. Rizzo was the flesh version of the archetypical movie cop: hard drinking, chain smoking himself into an early grave, divorced twice. He was approaching 50, but the drinking and smoking had taken their toll and he could have been mistaken for much older. Still, he was smart, tough, and Phil was glad he was on Joe's good side.

Phil felt he'd had it for one day. He was tired, hungry, and wanted nothing more than a quiet meal, a couple of beers, and whatever game was on that night.

The walk to his apartment on 45th Street usually took only ten minutes, but tonight he knew better than to count on the contents of his refrigerator, so he took the precaution of stopping in at the Imperial Dragon for some pork chow mein, figuring one order would be enough for him and Hank.

Chi Ho Chan, owner of the Imperial Dragon, greeted Phil as soon as he entered. "Oh, hello, Mr. Newland. So nice to see you. Will you be dining here or should we prepare something to take home?"

"Take home, Mr. Chan. One order of pork chow mein will be fine, thank you."

"Very good. It will be just a few minutes."

Mr. Chan, aware of Phil's situation, ordered the chow mein, but added an order of sweet and sour pork and a side of rice with a handful of fortune cookies.

When the food was ready, Phil looked at the bundle of cartons and knew it contained more than his one order of chow mein, although that was all he was charged for. Before leaving, he turned to look at Mr. Chan, who had been watching him from the kitchen entrance. Mr. Chan smiled and called out, "A little something for Hank." Phil knew there was no point in protesting; the truth was, he was grateful for the food and determined that he would more than pay for his order the next time he had occasion to spend some time in their kitchen.

Arriving at his apartment building, he found the elevator out of order, as usual, and, as usual, Phil told himself that he had to find better lodgings; then, of course, he remembered that better lodgings would cost more than what he could barely manage to scrape together for the dump he was in. Then too, would Hank move? The thought of leaving him behind was a painful consideration. And so Phil trudged up the three flights of stairs, with every step telling himself he could use the exercise and it was cheaper than a gym.

He unlocked the door to his apartment and went inside, flicking on the switch as he closed and locked the door behind him. He went through to the kitchen and put the cartons on the counter, then went to the living room window, opened it, and stepped aside as Hank, who had been waiting on the fire escape, leaped into the room and headed for the kitchen. With one mighty leap, he was on the counter and pawing at the cartons Phil had brought home.

Phil managed to push the stray cat he adopted aside long enough to retrieve one of the plastic containers he kept on hand for the purpose and, dropping in a scoopful of chow mein, put it and the cat on the floor; then he watched as Hank unceremoniously dug in.

Hank had come with the apartment, but no one had told Phil that he had inherited a feral cat that was anything but friendly. He first became aware of Hank's existence when he heard a God-awful wailing outside his living room window. Opening the window, he stuck his head out and found an emaciated tabby huddled on the fire escape. Since Phil's supper that evening happened to be his favorite pork chow mein and was all he had on hand, he put a cup full in the carton it came in and put it out on the landing. Hank did not move until Phil closed the window, at which point he lunged for the offering and demolished it, not stopping until the carton was empty, and then he licked it until it appeared brand new.

Little by little, and it was no mean feat, taking the better part of six months, but Phil gradually gained Hank's trust until the stray was willing to enter the apartment for his evening meal. Now it was their daily ritual. Phil either made or bought supper, put Hank's share in an empty container, and opened the living room window. Hank, who had been waiting outside, bounded inside and headed for his meal.

Over the course of their association, Hank endured Phil's attempts to make friends, even allowing himself to be petted as he ate. But once the meal was gone, Hank headed back to the window, where he would sit and moan until Phil let him out. Hank was actually one of Phil's considerations when he thought of moving, for he didn't think he could leave Hank behind; who else would feed him the Chinese dishes he had come to enjoy and look forward to?

Hank taken care of and gone as usual after eating, Phil saw to his own comforts. A plate of the chow mein, a can of whatever beer had been on sale that week, and Phil settled down to see what was on the tube, which he found himself only half listening to as his mind was on his client and the missing vase. In the morning, he would determine a course of action, and it would probably begin with an interview of the characters involved. That much decided, Phil relaxed with his meal, dealt with the few dishes he had used, and turned in, both excited and anxious about what the next day would bring.

The next morning, Phil treated himself to the sweet and sour pork for breakfast. He would have offered some to Hank, but Hank had already gone off on his daily rounds. Phil had no idea where the stray went, but he disappeared every morning before Phil was up and returned each evening in time for supper.

His day's agenda set, Phil dressed and left for his office. Once there, he called Georgia to see if she had any problem with him talking to her boss or the people in the shipping room. She didn't. In fact, she sounded grateful that someone was working on her behalf. That settled, he set off for the Worthington Gallery.

The gallery occupied a showroom, office, shipping room and warehouse in the Lawler Building on East 53rd, a building occupied by clothing and jewelry stores on the street level, with professional offices on the upper floors.

Harvey Worthington agreed to meet with Phil at nine o'clock and was waiting for him when he entered the showroom. Phil's first impression of the establishment was that it was a clean, efficient operation. Mr. Worthington greeted him warmly, offered him coffee and a chair across the desk from his own in the office.

A tall, well dressed and handsome man in perhaps his early forties, he essentially reiterated everything Georgia had already told him, emphasizing that the firm had an excellent reputation and the theft was the first real blemish on their record. He especially made clear that he did not believe Georgia was involved in any way. "Miss Redfield is an integral part of our operation and has always been in every way above reproach," he said. As they had when he had first seen Georgia, Phil's eyes automatically searched out Worthington's left hand. As with

Georgia, no wedding ring. Hmm—considering her boss's glowing defense of her character, the thought crossed Phil's mind that perhaps their relationship was something more than employer-employee.

"I understand, Mr. Worthington; but that was also my first impression of Miss Redfield. I believe she is truly upset over what happened; it never crossed my mind that she was involved in whatever happened to the original shipment. I would, however, like to talk to your shipping personnel, if that's all right with you."

"Certainly, Mr. Newland. Talk to anyone you choose, look at anything you like. We have nothing to hide and want to cooperate in any way we can to clear up this mess. And one other thing, please submit your bill directly to me when this is over; the firm will cover your expenses."

"Very well, I'll do that, sir," Phil told him, doing his best to hide his elation at the prospect of money actually coming in as the result of his efforts; it felt good.

With Worthington's approval, Phil headed for the shipping room. The first person he encountered was Mark Ripley, who was busily stuffing packing material around something in the box on the table in front of him; he was a tall kid with dark hair in a butch cut, kind of skinny, with a bad case of acne. Phil introduced himself and explained his presence at the gallery.

"Well, sure, Mr. Newland, I'll be happy to tell you whatever I know, but it's not much. I've just been working here for two weeks."

"I see," Phil said, disappointed that he apparently would not be able to talk to someone more familiar with the day-to-day operations of the shipping room.

"How did you get this job, Mark?" Phil asked, somehow immediately suspicious that the theft occurred at the same time as an apparent change of internal personnel.

"I was sent here by the employment office. The company needed someone in a hurry, didn't have time to go through the paper. The fellow I replaced had some kind of family trouble and couldn't give a long notice; actually, he just worked with me a couple of days before he left, so after that I just kind of had to get along and handle things as best I could. I think I'm doing all right, though. Tim, that is Tim Lawson, who was here before me, went over the general procedures—how things worked, who I should call for what, and so forth—and it really isn't so difficult once you get the hang of it."

"I see," Phil said, aware that he seemed to say that a lot. "Well then, tell me, Mark, did you handle the package Miss Redfield gave you, the one that was meant for Mr. Kandle?"

"I sure did. When the driver got here, I gave him the vase and insured it, just like she said I should. Mr. Newland, there was nothing wrong with anything we did here. However that vase went missing, it had to happen between here and Mr. Kandle. That's all I can tell you."

"Maybe not, Mark."

"What do you mean? What more can I say?"

"Well, Mark, if everything was copacetic here, as it sounds like it was, then we have to look at what happened when the vase left the gallery, and that starts with the driver who picked up the package and issued the insurance certificate."

"I told you. It was Apex, like always. Tim said they had used the same delivery company for as long as he worked here, and I guess he'd been here quite a while."

"Perhaps, but were you familiar with the driver? Was it the same person you usually dealt with?"

At this, Mark's eyes grew large. This was something he hadn't thought of. "Come to think of it," he said slowly, "as I recall it wasn't the same driver. I remember I mentioned it at the time, but the driver said the usual man was out sick and he was taking over his route for a few days. He was in uniform and had the right forms, seemed to know the procedures, I had no reason to question him, although now I wish I had. I should have called Apex and checked his story. Now that I recall,

I didn't even see his van, but then it was raining that day, bad storm; the back door was closed; I never even looked. I guess I was pretty stupid."

"No, Mark, not stupid. You may have just trusted the wrong person. But there is something else I'd like to ask you, if you don't mind?"

"Not at all. Shoot."

"Who made the call to Apex?"

Mark thought for a minute, then he said, "Come to think of it, Tim did. He said he'd give them a call since the package would be ready for pickup as soon as they could get here."

"And when did they get here?"

"About fifteen minutes later. Again, I didn't think much about it, figured they were just in the area when they got the call. I'm really sorry, Mr. Newland; I feel this is all my fault."

"No, it isn't, Mark, not at all, and I'll make sure Mr. Worthington knows that."

"Thanks, Mr. Newland."

Phil caught Mr. Worthington's attention in the gallery as he made his way out. "I've spoken to Mark," he told him, "and I don't feel this was in any way his fault. I believe this was all a carefully planned setup that counted on a new employee being unfamiliar with the Apex personnel. Do you have a minute for a few more questions?"

"Certainly, anything that will help clear this up. What would you like to know?"

"The fellow Mark replaced, how long was he with you?"

"About three months. Funny, but I would have thought we had stable personnel, yet all of a sudden Bill Merkle, who had been with us more than five years and ran the shipping room like clockwork, just didn't come in one day. When I called to find out what had happened, he just said he had found another job and had to start right away. That's when we hired Tim on Bill's recommendation. Then he didn't stay and now we have Mark."

"Well, your shipping room situation may have stabilized with Mark. I don't think whoever pulled this will get away with it again; if they try it, I think Mark has learned from this situation that he has to be suspicious and check anything that doesn't look or feel right."

"Thank you, Mr. Newland. What next?"

"I'd like what information you have on Bill Merkle and Tim Lawson. I'm going to do a little more checking on just how this spate of personnel turnovers got started."

Mr. Worthington disappeared into his office and returned a few minutes later with copies of both men's applications. With those in hand, Phil said, "I'll be in touch."

There was a small café a few doors down from the gallery, and Phil stopped in for a hamburger and coffee. Thus fortified, he put in a call to Sergeant Rizzo to update him on his progress and ask for background information on Tim Lawson. Phil thought it just a tad too convenient that Lawson was available to fill in for Bill Merkle on such short notice, and he thought he'd just have a talk with Merkle, too, and find out why a seemingly reliable employee would suddenly up and quit with no notice.

He took a bus uptown to Merkle's apartment building. He buzzed the apartment number and waited. And waited. Then he tried something he'd seen in a movie. He pressed all the apartment buzzers and waited again to see what would happen. The lock opened on the entrance door. The manager's door was between the entrance and the elevator, and Phil caught sight of it closing as he slipped inside. Now he approached the manager's apartment and rapped on the door. An elderly gentleman in tee shirt and coveralls answered, warily looking his visitor up and down. "What do you want?" he asked.

The name plate below the peephole said Ed Barber, so Phil said, "Mr. Barber, I'm looking for Bill Merkle. He didn't answer when I rang. Does he still live here?"

"Wish I knew, sonny," the old man wheezed. "Skipped out with three more months left on his lease. I can't rent it out if he's coming back, so I went inside to look around. He's gone. Took all his clothes, emptied his dresser and closet. Never said a word. Couldn't hardly believe it; he was one of my more reliable tenants, never any trouble and rent always paid on time. So I guess I can't help you none."

Phil didn't think there was any more he could do until he heard back from Rizzo on Lawson's background. In the meantime, he could go home and do his own research on the information he had on the two applications.

He decided against going to his office, figuring there was nothing he could do there that he couldn't do at home, so he arrived home earlier than he normally would have, but that was just fine. There were plenty of leftovers in the fridge for that night's supper. As soon as he reached the living room of his apartment, he opened the window as usual and waited for Hank to come bounding through. When the cat didn't appear immediately, Phil stuck his head out the window. He saw Hank huddled in a corner of the fire escape landing.

"Well, come on, Hank," he called. "Time for supper." At that, he watched as the cat slowly began to move and make his way toward the window, but something was wrong. Hank was limping. Phil waited while Hank slowly made his way through the open window, then he stopped the cat and tried to see what the trouble was. It didn't take long. There was a long bloody gash down the side of Hank's right rear leg. Phil examined it as well as he could, but it was clear it needed stitches, and his mind raced trying to think of the best thing to do. He didn't have money for a vet, he knew that much. But Hank needed help and there was no one else he could turn to.

Then he remembered a notice about a free vet clinic starting up over on Ramsey; he couldn't recall anything about hours, so he would just have to take a chance that he would find someone there. It was a good six block walk, so Phil wrapped the cat in a towel and started out.

They reached the clinic just as it was getting dark. Phil checked in with the receptionist and took a seat, Hank on his lap wrapped in the towel.

Looking around, Phil could see he was in a strictly no-frills operation. No magazines, no coffee, just a couple of beat-up end tables holding a couple of beat-up lamps. Beat-up chairs totaled six, five of which were occupied by two other cats, three non-descript dogs, and their owners, also looking beat up. Phil took the sixth chair and waited.

It took about an hour for the vet, a Doctor Garcia, to make his way through those ahead of Phil before his name was called.

The examining room was as beat up as the outer office, with everything having a donated look. Still, he wasn't there for the décor. Doctor Garcia carefully unwrapped the towel while he asked Phil what had happened. Phil said he didn't know, and explained that the cat was just a stray he had taken to feeding. He also said that while he thought Hank was normally a big, tough hombre, today he apparently met someone bigger and tougher.

Doctor Garcia smiled and said it looked like that was the case. He agreed the wound needed stitches and proceeded to put Hank to sleep. He cleaned the wound, put the stitches in and gave Hank a couple of shots. Then he told Phil that the cat should be kept inside for a few days and he wouldn't need to return because the stitches would eventually dissolve. Phil thanked him, wrapped Hank in the towel and started for the door. He noticed a box bolted to the wall requesting donations. He didn't have much, but probably had more than the others in the waiting room and the place couldn't run on air. He took out the biggest bill in his wallet, a crumpled ten, and dropped it in the box, then he and Hank headed home.

Once back in the apartment, Phil put Hank in the bathtub with a dish of the leftover chow mein and another dish of water. Then he left to see to his own supper, completely exhausted by his efforts on his case and his concern for Hank.

It was another forty-five minutes before Phil heard sounds from the bathroom. Hank was coming around. Phil petted him and told him to take it easy, that everything would be all right, and his supper was there if he was hungry. Hank's eyes were open, but he just laid on the bottom of the tub in his towel.

Phil wondered what else he could do, but just couldn't think of a thing. Then he did think of something Hank would need if he was to spend the night in the bathtub. Phil rummaged around in the basement of the apartment building until he found a box and some plants that someone had discarded. Upstairs, he cut the box down, lined the bottom with aluminum foil, and emptied the flower pots on top of the foil. It was the best he could do for a litterbox, but he was sure it would be sufficient. That done, he placed it on the bottom of the tub and once again tried to relax for the rest of the evening.

He dozed off after a while. When he woke up, he could hear Hank mewing in the bathroom. He jumped up and ran to see what was going on. Hank was out of his towel, his supper partially eaten, and the litterbox had served its purpose. Hank seemed to want out of the tub, but was unable to jump because of his injured leg. Phil very carefully picked him up and carried him to the living room, depositing him on a pillow on the sofa. The late show was just starting, so Phil got himself a beer and made himself comfortable beside the cat; after a while he could hear the distinct sound of purring. They stayed that way till morning.

Phil fried a couple of eggs for himself and shared these with Hank. He didn't share the toast, since Hank had never shown a fondness for it.

While he ate, Phil reviewed the applications he had gotten from the gallery. He found it interesting that Tim Lawson listed the manager of Oriental Imports, a Mr. Duane Barry, as a reference, along with Bill Merkle, who originally sent him to Worthington's gallery. Since Lawson didn't list Barry's import business as a former employer, Phil wondered what the connection was—just friends, or were they connected in some other way?

The phone book lay open on the table to the Uniforms section; Phil missed his secretary as he began dialing each in turn, beginning with those closest to the import business, to see if anyone had rented a blue delivery service uniform in the last month. He had no idea there were so many uniform sales and rental companies near the downtown area. It was slow going, as each business made him wait on hold while they checked their records. After two hours, all he had to show for his efforts was a series of "Sorry, but no."

During this time, Hank had begun making noises, so Phil picked him up from his place on the sofa and placed him back in the tub. The next time he looked, the last of yesterday's supper was gone and the litterbox had another deposit. After this, Hank attempted to exit the apartment his usual way via the window, but this time Phil explained to him that he was not to leave the apartment for a while—doctor's orders. Hank didn't like it, but since his sound effects were having no effects on Phil, he decided to make the best of things—for the time being.

Phil next put in a call to Sergeant Rizzo to compare notes. Joe found Lawson's connection to the import outfit as interesting as Phil did, but it was still just coincidence. They needed more.

His rundown of the uniform companies a bust, Phil had another idea—costume suppliers. Once again he ran down the costume shops in the area around the import business, looking for any rentals of a blue delivery outfit rented in the last month. This time the Kingston Party Outlet came through. They had indeed rented such an outfit three weeks ago to a woman, Marjorie Wilkins, who brought it back the next day.

Another call to Rizzo—who was Marjorie Wilkins?

Sergeant Rizzo's return call was very interesting indeed. Margorie Wilkins was employed as the office manager at Oriental Imports.

"By the way, Phil, you know that kid you asked me to look into, Tim Lawson?"

"Yes, you found something?"

"Maybe. It seems the kid was once arrested for shoplifting. Since it happened when he was still a juvenile, his parents were notified. His mother's maiden name was Barry."

The phone appeared to go dead. Rizzo thought they had lost the connection until he heard Phil say, "Barry, as in Duane Barry, as in Oriental Imports?"

"Yep. Duane's the uncle."

"This is almost too much, Joe. Certainly too much to be just a coincidence. Yet it doesn't seem the vase is really worth enough to make it worth all this subterfuge. What do you think?"

"I agree, Phil. There has to be more involved here than the twenty-five thousand the vase was appraised for. But what?"

"I wonder if a closer examination of Barry's import business might not be in order."

"Maybe. Let me talk to some friends in Customs and see what they think. I'll get back to you as soon as I have something."

"Sounds good. I hope this isn't just another dead end. Talk to you later."

Phil was stopped. Until he heard back from Rizzo, there was just nothing he could do. Well, actually, there was something he could do in the meantime, something he could and should have done earlier, but he had a feeling he knew the answer. He called Apex Freight and inquired about a pickup they had made at Worthington Gallery on the day the vase went missing. As he expected, they had no record of such a call. *Of course not.* When Lawson supposedly put in the call for pickup, it wasn't Apex he called, but the stooge they had rented the uniform for; it was he who showed up at the gallery with some phony papers they'd gotten from who knows where, and palmed both the phony messenger and insurance papers off on a new employee who wasn't that familiar with either. *Well, that loose end was taken care of.*

Next he called Mr. Chan at the Imperial Dragon.

"Ah, Mr. Newland. How very good to hear from you. How are you this find day?"

"I'm fine, Mr. Chan. I'm stalled on a case and was just wondering if you could use some extra help in your kitchen today or tomorrow."

"Yes, indeed, Mr. Newland. You come along. We will put you to work."

"Sounds good. I'll be there within the hour."

Before he left for the restaurant, Phil checked on Hank. He figured the bathtub was the safest place for the cat, so he made a bed for him of towels, replenished his food and water bowls, and tended to the litterbox. With all in order, he left for the Imperial Dragon.

It was the start of the dinner hour, and Chan's place was busy. Phil didn't need to be told what to do and jumped in like a buzzsaw. His specialty was the dishwasher. Manning that piece of equipment freed its usual operator for other kitchen chores like food prep, table bussing or counter work. Between take-outs and counter service, it was ten o'clock before Phil had a break, then another two hours to clean the kitchen and prepare for the next day, when he assured Mr. Chan he would be in right after breakfast. Phil left that night with cartons of kung pao chicken, wonton soup, and scallion pancakes.

The next morning, he and Hank shared the pancakes before Phil left for the restaurant. Mr. Chan didn't serve breakfast, but lunch hour started at eleven and the kitchen was a beehive of activity to make sure all ran smoothly. Phil found himself doing food prep and delivering lunch orders to businesses in the area; in the afternoon it was back to the dishes, his day rounded out with a quick mop up of the kitchen floor and a trip to the backyard dumpster with the day's garbage. Once again cartons were hauled home for himself or dropped off at a nearby homeless shelter.

Phil had told Mr. Chan he didn't know when he would be able to be back as he was waiting for information before he could proceed on a case he was working on. Mr. Chan was grateful for the help Phil was able to give him, as restaurant work was hard and not many were willing to do what had to be done to keep the orders moving; fortunately his gratitude went beyond the cartons of excess food he always sent home with Phil, for Mr. Chan also paid him the going wage for any hours he worked.

Hank was healing nicely, but Phil was reluctant to let him out after what happened. Yet he didn't know if Hank would tolerate living entirely indoors.

Phil returned to his office to catch up on his mail. He was sorting his bills into pay and delay stacks when his phone rang; he got a lift when he heard Sergeant Rizzo's voice.

"Phil, I talked to some contacts in Customs and DEA. It seems they've had Oriental Imports in their sights for some time. After all, what better setup for smuggling anything at all than an import business, but they never had enough cause to give him a real going over—until now. With the theft of the vase, Barry's nephew, and the phony pickup agent, they decided to give his place a closer look. They went in with a search warrant yesterday, of course that was just the cover. But it was enough. They found your vase, along with enough other illegal artifacts, not to mention a drug stash, along with Barry's contact list of people that made some nice additions to their own surveillance list. Mr. Barry's operation will be out of commission for the very lengthy foreseeable future."

Phil listened in disbelief, then said, "But Joe, all for a vase? If he wanted the thing so badly, why didn't he just steal it? Why go through all the phony Apex bit, why involve his nephew, and why would the nephew even agree to be a part of all that nonsense?"

"We asked the same questions. It seems the nephew had been using his gig at the gallery to keep his uncle clued in to new arrivals on the watch list they kept of international collectors who weren't too particular about how they got their goodies. Worthington had the usual imports, all perfectly legal with papers to back them up. He was a legitimate dealer, but that was the problem. He never dealt in the kinds of artifacts that would appeal to the clientele Barry catered to. Until the vase showed up.

"Tim Lawson didn't recognize it, he just took a picture and passed it along to his uncle. But when Barry saw it, his eyes lit up with dollar signs. The vase was a rare type of rose jade from the Ming period and was known among collectors as the Rose Key. Barry knew it would set off a feeding frenzy among the few truly serious collectors who would literally pay almost anything to get their hands on it. Barry was afraid just stealing it would be too ham handed and he'd be the first one suspected. But somehow he had the wacky idea that if the vase, the phony Apex driver, and his nephew all just disappeared, he could somehow hid in the confusion long enough to exchange the vase for some very serious cash."

"But how did he arrange for such a swift and convenient exchange of personnel?"

"Not that hard. The original shipping clerk, Bill Merkle, really did have a family emergency. Seems they had a family business; then his father had a heart attack. The kid had to take over; that it happened at a particularly convenient time for Barry was just coincidence. The nephew, Tim Lawson, was paid off and simply told to get lost; Barry didn't ask him where he was going and didn't want to know, in case it came up on a lie detector. And as for Marjorie Wilkins, it seems she was simply expendable; I guess office managers aren't that hard to come by."

"Unbelievable," Phil said. "But having his office manager rent the uniform? Did he really think nobody would notice?"

"What can I tell you? The smartest crooks often do the stupidest things. On the other hand, maybe it's only stupid if she connects Barry to the idea, because right now she's AWOL, probably split when you started nosing around, and Barry claims he has no idea where she went. But until, or unless, she turns up, he can claim everything was her idea, that she ran the entire operation, and he just signed whatever she put in front of him."

"I don't imagine she'll be easy to find, alive anyway?"

"No idea, Phil; no idea at all."

"So, when can the gallery get their vase back?"

"Right now it's evidence, but I don't see why a picture wouldn't do just as well. I'll see what I can do."

"Okay. Thanks, Joe."

"Don't mention it. We're here to serve."

Phil took a few minutes to digest Joe's information, and then put in a call to Harvey Worthington. After listening to his recount of the activities of the various authorities involved in surveillance of Duane Barry's import business, Mr. Worthington told him, "I'm simply incredulous, Mr. Newland, at the extent to which his tentacles reached, and all discovered because of your investigation. We owe you a great deal and I'm sure I speak for Miss Redfield when I tell you we are very grateful."

"Thank you," Phil told him. "Once the vase is returned to you, you can forward it to Mr. Kandle none the worse for wear."

"We'll let him know the piece is safe and will shortly be on its way to him."

That done, Phil turned his attention to the matter of his expenses. After recounting his fees and activities on behalf of the gallery, Phil submitted his bill to Mr. Worthington as the man requested. And then he waited.

The day after dropping his bill off at the gallery, Phil heard a knock at his office door. Opening it, there was a messenger from a courier service with a large envelope for him. Phil signed for it and closed the door. Opening the outer envelope, Phil found another letter-sized envelope inside. Opening this, he found a letter from Mr. Worthington thanking him for his efforts and reiterating the firm's gratitude. Enclosed with the letter was a check in the full amount of the expenses he had submitted. The man never quibbled about the amount or questioned any of the items it covered.

Phil sat looking at both the letter and the check for a long time. It had been a long while since his agency had any profits and he had to decide on how best to allot the funds the check covered. Thinking it over, Phil decided to pay the cleaning service what he owed them and see what he could do about returning his office to some degree of order. Then, he would put enough away to cover his rent for the next two months for his office and apartment, thus being assured of both a professional address and a home for himself and Hank.

That pretty much ate up the proceeds that looked so good just a few minutes earlier. *Oh well, easy come, easy go.* But it started Phil to thinking about just how precarious his situation really was. Except for the check from the gallery, and he just thanked his lucky stars that Mr. Worthington was an honorable man who paid his debts promptly, his only income was from the Imperial Dragon. He didn't like being one Chinese restaurant away from homelessness.

He had to find another gig to supplement his income from his own agency, which before this latest caper had been close to non-existent.

He was contemplating his situation while staring at the wall of his next-door neighbor when his phone rang. Still deep in thought, Phil answered and simply said, "Hello." A man's voice on the other end of the line said, "I'm looking for Mr. Philip Newland. Is he there?"

Phil almost dropped the phone when he managed to answer, "Yes, I'm Phil Newland. I'm sorry for being a little preoccupied, but I just spilled my coffee and was mopping it up when the phone rang. Again, I'm very sorry. Now then, how can I help you?"

"Mr. Newland, my name is Jim Hoyt. I have a small electronic supply company here in town. We are a specialty supplier and ship all over the country and have had a few international shipments as well."

"I see," Phil said, although he really didn't. "But what has this to do with me?"

"Well, it's like this: We have had a problem recently with supplies disappearing. At first, because they were often small parts, we thought they had just been mislaid somewhere in our plant. But it's been happening too often for this to be simple carelessness. It has to be theft, but I have neither the time or the know how to track it down. I want you to find out who is responsible and how they are operating. We have about forty employees, any one of whom could have pocketed the parts, or hidden them, or misdirected them, I simply don't know. Can you help us?"

Phil digested all the man told him, all the while trying to tamp down the excitement he felt at the prospect of another case. Then he said, "Mr. Hoyt, may I ask how you happened to contact me?"

"Oh, I'm sorry. Harvey Worthington told me about your efforts on his behalf. When I told him of my own troubles, he suggested I contact you to discuss the matter. Harvey is my half-brother."

"I see," Phil said again, aware that he was being redundant. "In that case, I'd be happy to look into the matter for you, Mr. Hoyt. If you'll just give me some information, I'll see what we can do."

"Great. Harvey said I could count on you. We'll cooperate in any way we can. Just tell me what you need."

"Well, first of all, I'd rather you didn't mention my involvement to anyone, and don't change your normal activities in any way. It will only put the culprit on guard and we don't need that."

"I understand. Right now Harvey is the only person I've talked to and I know I can depend on him to keep things quiet."

"Yes, I think so, too," Phil answered. "Give me a few days to gather some background information I'll need to figure out the most sensible course of action, then I'll contact you and we'll get to work."

"Sounds good. I'll be waiting to hear from you, and thank you."

"My pleasure, Mr. Hoyt. Talk to you soon."

At home that evening, Phil and Hank dined on the sweet and sour pork and rice that had been waiting in the refrigerator, topped off with an obligatory can of beer in front of the TV. Since being injured, Hank had turned into quite the homebody, content to spend his time lazing on the sofa and listening to the radio that Phil left on to keep him company.

That night, Phil told Hank all about his new case, while Hank listened intently, purring in response.

"You know, Hank, I've got a good feeling about this case. It's a referral. At last, someone thought enough of my efforts to recommend me to someone they knew. What do you think of that?"

Hank stretched, arching his back against Phil's leg. Taking this movement as a signal of Hank's approval, Phil simply said, "I see."

-The End -

Also by Amanda Brenner

Sid Langdon Mysteries
Tainted Legacy
The Cottage by the Lake
The Mystery of the Nourdon Blue

Standalone
Call to Duty
Temporarily Away
The Case of the Pilfered Painting
Covenant of Blood
Shadow of the Rope
Trail of Vengeance
While My Love Sleeps
Dustup At Deadhorse
A Change of Plan
Jaded
The Last Cookie
Collected Short Stories Of Mystery, Romance, And The Occult

Watch for more at pillaredroses.webs.com.

About the Author

Amanda Brenner is a native Midwesterner who has traveled extensively throughout the United States and now lives quietly with her husband and an assortment of wildlife visitors to their urban home. Her interest in writing began at an early age when westerns were popular attractions at the local theater. It seemed only natural that her first novel, Trail of Vengeance, should be in that genre. After finishing a second western, Shadow of the Rope, she began to explore a new direction and completed three contemporary mysteries involving private investigator Sid Langdon, a self-doubting magnet for offbeat clients and hapless scenarios, the latest being The Mystery of the Nourdon Blue. Amanda enjoys learning from the books she reads, a characteristic reflected in the research she includes in her own works.

Thank you for your time.

Read more at pillaredroses.webs.com.

www.ingramcontent.com/pod-product-compliance
Lightning Source LLC
Chambersburg PA
CBHW071519150726
48000CB00002B/606